"Do you really believe I'm blackmailing Roger?"

"I don't know what to believe. I know virtually nothing about you, thanks to your total failure to communicate!"

"We communicated last night, Kelsey."

"That's your idea of communication?" she yelped, leaping to her feet as her emotions threatened to overwhelm her. "You're out of your mind. What in heaven's name made me think we could ever develop a long-term relationship? Forget last night, Cole. It's past history, and we don't talk about past history, remember? I only want to know what you're doing to Roger."

"I'm not doing anything to him."

"Are you blackmailing him?" she demanded.

The gray gaze was as cold as the ocean on a winter's day. "What do you think?"

"Jayne Ann Krentz entertains to the hilt..."
—Catherine Coulter

JAYNE ANN KRENTZ

Man with a PAST

ISBN 1-55166-624-3

MAN WITH A PAST

Copyright © 1985 by Jayne Ann Krentz.

Visit us at www.mirabooks.com

Printed in U.S.A.

Man with a
PAST

ONE

This was the night she would have to tell him she was not going to see him again.

Kelsey Murdock stood in front of the floor-to-ceiling windows of her mother's beachfront home and gazed thoughtfully out into the darkness. It was raining again tonight. Not an unusual state of affairs during winter here on California's Monterey Peninsula. The weather fitted her mood she decided: quiet, meditative, vaguely regretful for what might have been.

But she was convinced of the rightness of the decision she had made. She'd played with fire long enough. If she didn't stop now she would very likely get burned.

Cole Stockton, the man she mentally labeled "fire," came up behind her, moving with the soundless stride she sometimes found intriguing and at other times unnerving. It didn't seem normal for a man to move with such hushed control.

"When your mother and stepfather return from their trip to New Zealand we'll have to find other excuses for your weekend visits," Cole remarked in the quiet, dark voice that matched the way he moved. "You won't be able to say you're just coming down to Carmel to water the plants and check the mail for your parents while they're away."

"No," she agreed, accepting the glass of Armagnac he had poured for her. Kelsey sipped the fine brandy and told herself she would wait a little longer before she explained that she wouldn't be needing any more excuses to make the drive from San Jose to Carmel. After tonight her only reason for the trip would be that of the occasional visit to her mother and stepfather. And as much as she loved her mother, Amanda, and liked the man her mother had married, she certainly had no intention of spending every weekend here in Carmel visiting them!

"You're very quiet," Cole observed as she turned to face him. He didn't smile at her as he raised the balloon-shaped glass to his mouth. Cole Stockton rarely smiled. But there was an expression of warm anticipation in his smoky-gray eyes.

"It's been a busy week at work." Kelsey excused her mood lightly, but inwardly she experienced a small frisson of uneasiness. With a sudden flash of feminine intuition she knew exactly what he was thinking. Tonight he intended to end the cautious, intricate dance of sensual attraction in which they had been engaged for the past month. Tonight Cole intended to take her to bed.

It was ironic, she thought, that Cole had decided to make his move the same evening she had made up her mind to end the dangerous relationship. He would not be pleased, but surely at his age he had learned the deal with rejection. After all he must be close to forty.

But it was almost as difficult to pinpoint Cole Stockton's age as it was to nail down anything else about the man. It was her inability to learn anything other than the most superficial facts about him that had led Kelsey to her decision to end the relationship before it became any more involved.

A man who, even under the most delicate probing, would reveal nothing of his past, who showed no interest in the long-term future, who calmly provided no explanation for his apparent financial security, who would discuss only the present as though he had materialized out of nowhere less than a year ago, such a man obviously did not believe in the kind of honest, open relationship in which Kelsey believed. The only wise course of action was to end the association before it could develop into a full-blown affair.

Mentally Kelsey cataloged the few obvious facts she did know about Cole. He was a friend of her stepfather's, she realized, but Roger Evans didn't seem to know anything more about him than did anyone else. It was obvious he genuinely liked the younger man. So did her mother, Amanda, for that matter. They had introduced Kelsey and Cole a month ago, shortly before leaving on their trip to New Zealand.

In addition to the knowledge that her parents liked their neighbor, Kelsey also knew that Cole had money. At least enough to afford one of the expensive beachfront houses here near Carmel. She had seen the outside of his home since he'd had the stone walls built, but for some reason she hadn't wanted to go inside. On the two occasions this past month when he'd suggested having dinner at his place she had graciously refused.

He hadn't objected when she'd neatly reversed the offers, inviting him to dine with her at her parents' house, instead, and Kelsey hadn't been forced to deal with the fact that she felt uncomfortable with the idea of entering the massive wrought-iron gate that opened onto his walled fortress of a home. It was as though a primitive part of her feared being trapped inside.

Probably the most arresting thing about Cole Stockton was his attitude of quiet watchfulness. He always seemed alert and aware, even when he was relaxing with a drink in his hand, as he was tonight.

There was a harsh strength stamped on his unhandsome face that Kelsey found far more riveting than conventional good looks. It also proclaimed a past, even though Cole flatly refused to acknowledge one. The smoke-gray eyes were normally as unreadable as everything else about the man. The only emotion Kelsey could be certain of in those fog-colored depths was blatant masculine desire, and even that was well-controlled, as always, this evening. The cordovan brown pelt of his hair was sleekly cut with a conservative razor.

Tonight Cole wore a black pullover of fine wool and a pair of black slacks. Both garments fitted his lean, smoothly muscled body well. Kelsey's mouth lifted in wry amusement as a thought struck her.

"Something's amusing you?" Cole inquired politely.

"I just realized you nearly always wear dark colors

at night. Stand you outside on a rainy evening like this
and you'd disappear into the background."

"I wasn't planning on standing outside in the rain."

"Do you even own a white shirt? Or a red one? I've
never seen you in anything but khaki, browns and
greens during the day and black at night."

"A limited wardrobe, I'm afraid. Perhaps I should
take out a subscription to *Gentlemen's Quarterly?*"

He mocked her gently, but Kelsey realized he was
faintly puzzled by the hint of annoyance in her tone.
Criticizing the remarkably neutral colors of his clothing was ridiculous, and she knew it. But it was just one
more tiny, unexplained aspect of his life she knew she
would never be allowed to question. In a way it was
the last straw. After a month of weekend dates she had
had it with trying to dig beneath the surface of Cole
Stockton. If he wanted to wear colors that allowed him
to blend in with his surroundings, night and day, let
him!

"I'm sorry," she murmured coolly. "That was rather
rude of me."

"You're feeling quite tense tonight, aren't you? Was
the week really that bad?"

"There was a lot to be done before I leave on my vacation week after next," she hedged, turning back to
the window. Cole's quietly intimidating presence was
disturbing her more than she wanted to admit. Perhaps because she had made up her mind she would
not be seeing him again. A perverse part of her would
always wonder what it would have been like to lose
herself, however briefly, in an affair with Cole Stockton.

At least she would have the consolation of knowing it could never have amounted to more than an affair. A man like this one would never allow a woman anywhere near as intimate a relationship as marriage, she thought bitterly. She was giving up only the prospect of a short-term passion, not a long-lived, caring relationship.

"I've been thinking about that Caribbean cruise you've booked," Cole said slowly, glancing down into the rich Armagnac as he swirled it gently in the glass.

"What about it?" Kelsey only half listened, her mind on when and how she would tell him that this was their last evening together.

"There's no reason I couldn't come along," Cole mused.

Kelsey's breath caught in her throat as she considered that prospect. "The cruise was nearly sold out months ago. I was lucky to get reservations myself."

"I could always share your stateroom," he remarked, gray eyes gleaming with unsubtle male promise.

Kelsey forced a distant smile, determinedly squelching the small burst of panic that had flared to life in the pit of her stomach. "I don't think so."

"You might change your mind by the time you're scheduled to leave."

He didn't move, but she had the impression he had stalked a little closer. Kelsey resisted the impulse to back away. "Has anyone ever mentioned you have a tendency to be rather arrogant at times?"

Cole didn't respond to that. But, then, he seemed to find it easy to ignore questions he didn't wish to answer. Instead he watched her quietly for a moment, absently tasting his brandy. "You think that by the time you leave you won't be ready to share a bedroom with me?" he finally inquired, far too silkily.

Now was the moment to tell him she would never be ready to share a bedroom with him. But for some reason Kelsey hesitated, foolishly wanting to keep the evening alive just a little while longer. There wouldn't be any more of these charming, intriguing, frustrating weekends after tonight, and she was reluctant to bring them to an end. "Perhaps we should try discussing another subject," she suggested with an ease she was far from feeling.

"All right. How about your hectic week?"

Kelsey lifted one shoulder gracefully beneath the fire-red material of her dress. The close-fitting knit, with its long sleeves and tiny gold buttons down the front, gently outlined the small curves of her breasts, a slender waist and the flare of womanly thighs. She was five feet four inches and even with the high heels she had on tonight she was unable to meet Cole on an equal level. He was a notch under six feet, and in addition to the height, she knew she could never hope to match the lean, coordinated strength of him. It occurred to her to question whether she need fear that strength. Surely he would not lose control just because she told him she wouldn't be seeing him again. She seriously doubted there was much in the world that could make Cole lose control.

Then again, she knew so damn little about the man!

"My week really wasn't all that bad," she began determinedly, "just a lot to accomplish. My boss is set on finishing some important documents before I leave so that I can hand carry them to that flaky genius I told you about."

"The one who lives like a recluse on some Caribbean island?"

"Right. I'm going to go ashore at one of the scheduled cruise stops, hop a charter flight to the kook's private island and deliver the papers personally. The charter pilot will fly me right back to the port where the ship is docked. Shouldn't be any problem, and I'll get an interesting side trip out of it. Walt said my vacation was a case of perfect timing. If I hadn't been going on the cruise he would have had to pay another courier's fee. Whenever he sends business material to this guy he has to make certain it's hand carried."

"This way Gladwin has to pick up the tab for only a short charter hop between islands," Cole growled. "It would seem that, in addition to his other sterling qualities, Walt Gladwin is a bit cheap."

In spite of the growing tension, Kelsey allowed herself a quick grin, her near-green eyes sparkling with momentary mischief. "You've never liked Walt, and yet you haven't even met the man!"

"Maybe I just don't care for the way his name seems to come up so frequently in our conversations."

The humor faded from Kelsey's eyes. "I won't mention him again."

"Don't make rash promises," Cole advised dryly. "He's your boss, and since we discuss your work a great deal, I'm sure his name will continue to crop up."

"If I talk too much about my job at Flex-Glad perhaps it's because you never seem to want to discuss your work," she retorted crisply.

Cole lifted an eyebrow in vague surprise. "I'm willing to talk about what I do for a living, it's just that my various investment strategies always seem a little dull compared to your high-tech work. At Flex-Glad you're really on the cutting edge of the new computer technology."

"I'm a glorified secretary," Kelsey said wryly. "It's true my title sounds a little more prestigious, but I assure you that administrative assistants spend a lot of time running errands, putting out fires and convincing temperamental computer whizzes to cooperate with management in creating a marketable product. I don't do any of the real technical work. I just try to coordinate those who can do it and those who are trying to market it."

"You know something about the technical side of things. Look at the way you helped your stepfather set up his new home computer."

Kelsey shrugged. "You can't help but pick up a few things here and there when you work around the technical stuff all day long, I suppose. Frankly, I'd much rather hear about your investments. Is that really what you do all week long? Follow the *Wall Street Journal?*"

"That and several other economic news sources. I have a lot to learn, though. In fact, I've been thinking of having you help me set up a home computer like Roger's."

Kelsey refused to be sidetracked. "How long have you been managing your investments on a full-time basis?" she pressed, trying for any small hint of his past that she could get.

"Almost a year."

"And before that? What did you do before moving to the Monterey Peninsula?"

His eyes narrowed consideringly, and she knew he was weighing every word, selecting the point at which he would cut off the flow of information about himself. It was always this way.

"I acquired the money I now have to invest," he offered calmly.

"How?"

"Here and there."

Blank wall again. Kelsey had known it would be there, of course. She was accustomed to running headlong into it. Every time she pushed for information that went further into his past than the year he had spent in the Carmel area she hit that barricade. Well, she assured herself bracingly, after tonight she wouldn't have to worry about it.

"Did you inherit your money, Cole?" she couldn't resist asking.

"No." He stepped closer and touched the tawny-brown sweep of her hair where it fell in a smooth, styled curve on her shoulders. "Let's talk about something else, Kelsey. The past doesn't interest me. Only the present. I've told you that."

"Several times," she agreed, stifling a small sigh. There was no point probing further. He would turn aside every question. Since this would be their last evening together she might as well endeavor to make it a pleasant one. With a bright smile she toasted him. "To the future."

His gaze roved over her. "To the present," he amended, raising his glass in an echoing salute. "Especially tonight. I've learned that the here and now is all you can really count on in life." Cole put the rim of his glass to Kelsey's lips and tipped it gently so that she was forced to take a small sip. Then, his eyes never leaving hers, he took a swallow of the brandy, setting his mouth to the same place on the glass that hers had touched.

Kelsey felt the heat of his implied intent. Her fingers tightened around her glass as she realized she was trembling slightly. "Speaking of tonight," she began quietly.

"A much more interesting topic than last year or next year."

"Yes, well, it's getting rather late, isn't it," Kelsey tried to say briskly.

"You didn't get here until rather late."

"The traffic out of San Jose was terrible," she explained quickly. "You know how it is on Friday afternoons. The freeways are jammed."

"Fortunately that's one of the aspects of modern life with which I don't have to contend. Living here on the peninsula has some definite advantages," Cole murmured. There was a pause before he went on deliberately, "But I suffer from the effects of your traffic problems in some ways."

"How?"

"I have to spend Friday afternoons waiting for you,

never knowing just how late you'll be. And I worry about your driving."

"But I'm an excellent driver," Kelsey said in surprise. It hadn't occurred to her he might have been worried. The man didn't seem capable of such a useless emotion as worry.

"I've got news for you. Knowing you think you're a good driver does not keep me from being concerned," he told her dryly.

She wasn't certain how to take that. After all, this was the last weekend it would be a problem for him. "Any suggestions? Roller skates, perhaps?"

"I do have a few ideas on the subject I'd like to discuss with you," Cole said evenly.

"I'm listening." Her gaze focusing on the darkness beyond the windows, Kelsey was conscious of Cole collecting his words before he spoke. It was as if he wanted to approach this next bit very carefully.

"How important is your job to you?"

Startled by the question, Kelsey slanted him a curious glance over her shoulder. "It puts food on the table and gas in the car. It pays the rent and the taxes. I guess you could say it was very important."

"I could pay for all those things," Cole told her softly.

Kelsey froze. "You could what?"

"You heard me. Kelsey, I want you to think about moving in with me." There was a steady determination in his words that told Kelsey he meant them.

"Is this some kind of joke?" she whispered shakily. "We've known each other exactly one month. And during that time we've only seen each other on the weekends!"

"I'm not going to rush you," Cole soothed. "I just want you to start thinking about it. A long-distance arrangement would eventually be a strain on both of us."

"Yes," she agreed bitterly. "It would."

"Kelsey, have I upset you?"

"If I'm upset I have no one but myself to blame."

Cole slid his hand under the curve of her hair, fitting his palm to the nape of her neck as he gently forced her to turn and face him. "You're as tense as a strung bow tonight, honey," he said, stroking the sensitive area.

"Sorry, maybe it has something to do with the lack of romance in your little offer." Angrily she stepped out from under his hand. "Asking a woman to give up her job and move in as a full-time mistress is considered tacky in this day and age, Cole. I think it was always considered tacky. Did you honestly expect me to jump at the idea?"

"Calm down," he said softly, a thread of command in his voice.

And it was a real command, Kelsey decided fleetingly. Not just a warning. "I'm not becoming hysterical. Merely annoyed."

"I've told you I won't rush you."

"You're right. You won't rush me. In fact you will wait indefinitely. Cole, the last thing I'm ever going to do is give up my job."

"You're overreacting," he accused grimly. "I'm not asking you to give up your financial independence."

"No? That's what it sounded like to me!"

"Even if you stopped working tomorrow you'd still

have your inheritance, wouldn't you? Or have you spent it all?"

She stared at him. "My 'inheritance'! What in the world are you talking about?"

He frowned. "Your mother happened to mention once that when she inherited her brother's estate there was a certain amount earmarked for you."

Kelsey was torn between fury and outright laughter. "Did she tell you just how much money I received from Uncle Curtis? I got exactly ten thousand dollars. Cole, that's not even a year's salary for me. How long do you think I could be financially independent on that? If you were thinking of getting your hands on my 'fortune,' better revise your plans. I'm not an heiress."

His fingers knotted around the snifter and the gray gaze became a swirl of ice crystals. "You know damn well I never had any such intentions."

"I hardly know you at all," she retorted bleakly. "How could I guess what your intentions might or might not be?"

"For God's sake, Kelsey, at least tell me you don't really think I was angling to get control of your money," he gritted.

In spite of her tension and resentment, Kelsey had the grace to back down on that issue. If there was one thing of which she was instinctively certain, it was that Cole had far too much pride to live off a woman. "Of course I don't think that," she said, relenting. "You're right. I am a little tense tonight."

"I honestly believed you had received enough from your uncle to enable you to feel financially independent. Your mother has implied you only work because you'd be bored otherwise."

Humor flashed in Kelsey's eyes. "My mother has been indulging herself in something of a fantasy world ever since she inherited this house and the income from my uncle's estate. She had to work long and hard to support me after my father died. Occasionally Uncle Curtis would condescend to send us a small check at Christmas, but that was all the help he ever gave her. He had never approved of my father, you see, and more or less felt my mother had got what she deserved for marrying an artist."

"Your father was an artist?"

"An unsuccessful one, I'm afraid." Kelsey smiled. "A dreamer. He was a lot of fun at times, but he wasn't a very good husband or father. He lived waiting to be discovered, and it never happened. He died when I was twelve. My mother really had a struggle on her hands holding things together financially. Five years ago when Uncle Curtis died she suddenly had money for the first time in her life. She's been enjoying it enormously. Trips to Europe, this lovely home and a wonderfully debonair, courtly new husband. She's having a great time and I'm very happy for her. But the truth is, she has very little control over the money. It's all invested, and by the terms of the will she can only live off the income. The estate is managed by my uncle's bank. My mother has the use of the income for her lifetime, and then the money goes to my uncle's favorite charities. Uncle Curtis didn't want to destroy my ambition by leaving me too much money too young," she concluded on a note of laughter.

Cole appeared to turn the situation over several times in his mind, and then he nodded. "Okay, so suggesting you give up your job is asking a lot. I understand that. But I'm prepared to make up for the financial loss. I'll take good care of you, Kelsey. Believe me, I can easily afford it. I could even pay you the equivalent of your present salary if that would give you a feeling of financial security."

Kelsey closed her eyes in silent disgust. "You're serious, aren't you?"

"Completely. I've thought about this a great deal."

She shook her head wonderingly. "Where have you been for the past ten years, Cole? The world doesn't work that way anymore."

"The hell it doesn't," he countered softly. "I want you and I think you want me. Your job is in the way because it separates us geographically. I have more than enough money for both of us. All that adds up to a very neat conclusion."

"Which is that I quit my job and move in with you?"

"Why not?" he asked earnestly. "If you really want to work in order to keep from being bored you can get involved with my investments. Or you can find something to do in Carmel."

"Open another cutesy boutique like the dozens of others that are already there?"

"Kelsey," he began warningly.

Rage simmered in Kelsey's veins. She controlled it with a supreme effort of will. "There's another alternative."

"What's that?" he demanded warily.

"You could move to San Jose."

It was his turn to eye her searchingly and ask, "Are you serious?"

"Why not?" she shot back flippantly. "Your work would appear to be more portable than mine."

"You'd rather live in San Jose when you could live here on the beach?" he taunted. "You would prefer the traffic and the smog and the crime and all the rest? Come on, Kelsey, you know as well as I do that you love this area."

"Everyone loves Carmel and the Monterey Peninsula," she tossed back icily. "But not everyone can afford to live here. You can afford it, and so can my mother and Roger. But I'm not in the same financial boat as the rest of you. It would probably take months for me to find another job around here. The odds are it wouldn't pay nearly as much or be nearly as interesting as the one I have now."

"I've just told you I can take care of you."

"And I've been trying to explain to you that I don't intend to become a professional mistress!"

Cole surveyed her flushed features and appeared to come to a quick conclusion. "I'm pushing too hard, too soon," he said soothingly. "I'm sorry, Kelsey. There's no need for us to have this argument tonight. And I certainly don't want to ruin the rest of the weekend. Let me have your glass. I'll get you some more of your stepfather's Armagnac. I'll say one thing for Roger, he knows his brandy. I shall have to buy him another bottle to replace the one you and I have been working on for the past month."

Before Kelsey could think of a logical protest, Cole had deftly removed the snifter from her hand. She watched nervously as he walked silently across the hardwood floor and the elegant Oriental carpet to pick up the bottle of French brandy that resided on a teak table. This wasn't going to get any easier, she thought morosely.

He had shaken her with his outrageous suggestion that she give up everything and become his concubine. It was alarming to discover that Cole had plunged ahead in his plans for their uncertain relationship. In her mind they were very much at the beginning of an association that, given time and appropriate circumstances, might have blossomed into something meaningful. She realized now that in Cole's mind the affair was an assumed fact. He was already planning the practical details.

"You look confused and very annoyed with me," Cole remarked as he glanced back over his shoulder at her. "There's no need for either emotion. Not tonight. I'm not going to rush you, Kelsey. I know you've grown accustomed to your independence. After all, you're what? Twenty-eight?"

She nodded, wondering where all this was heading.

"And you've been on your own a long time."

"Ever since high school," she agreed cautiously. "I worked my way through college."

"And you've never been married," he went on, carrying her brandy back across the room. "So you've never had to adjust your life-style to anyone else's, have you?"

"I've never been any man's kept woman, if that's what you mean," she flared.

"It's not what I mean," he growled. "And you know

it. Haven't you ever made a commitment to a man, Kelsey? Surely you've cared about someone sometime during the past twenty-eight years!"

"Of course," she tried to say carelessly.

"Well?" he challenged. "Go on. Didn't you learn anything from the experience?"

"Only that you may be right about long-distance relationships," she said coolly, turning her back to him as she sipped the brandy.

"What's that supposed to mean?"

Why should she tell him, she wondered angrily. He had no right to pry into her past. Not when he refused to answer even the most superficial questions about his own background. She didn't have to let him dredge up that fiasco with Aaron Blake. She had put it firmly behind her, telling herself that all she needed to remember about it was the lesson it had taught her.

"A couple of years ago I was madly in love with a man who did a lot of traveling," she heard herself say stonily. "He was an executive with a firm back in the Midwest and he did business with the company where I worked. We could only see each other when his business brought him to town, but he made certain that was as frequently as possible. He was quite happy to let me adjust my schedule to his. Quite happy to let me make the commitment. And I was only too happy to do it." Kelsey inclined her head in self-mocking humor.

"Things didn't work out, I take it?" Cole asked roughly.

"No."

"Because the distance factor made a meaningful relationship impossible? Kelsey, that's just what I'm trying to tell you—"

"No!" she interrupted fiercely. "It wasn't just that there was a lot of geography between us, although I'm sure that eventually would have been a problem. It was that there were a lot of lies between us. The fact that we lived so far apart merely made it easier for him to hide those lies."

Behind her she could feel Cole going very still. "What kind of lies?"

"He was married," she explained bluntly. "It was months before I found out. Someone at work had to be the one to enlighten me. God, I felt like such a fool!"

"What did you do then?"

Kelsey yanked her mind away from the bitter, humiliating memories and tried to concentrate on the point of the story. "I quit my job because I couldn't stand having to see him on a business basis after that. I also got the pleasure of telling him what I thought of him. Other than a severe lesson on the importance of trust and honesty in a relationship, that was about all I did get out of the mess. Don't tell me I don't know what it's like adjusting my life-style to someone else's. Aaron Blake forced me to do some really major adjusting, including finding a new job!"

"Kelsey, everything you've just told me points to what I've been trying to explain this evening. Conducting an affair over long distance will be very hard on both of us. Aside from the fact that I already miss you during the week, there's the problem I'm developing worrying about that drive from San Jose on Friday evenings. I also don't like wondering where the hell you are when I call during the week and you don't answer the phone," he added with a sudden emphasis that told its own story.

Kelsey tilted her head. "I didn't know you called this past week."

His mouth twisted wryly. "Tuesday, Wednesday and Thursday evenings, to be exact. You were out all three times."

She reflected briefly, inordinately pleased that he had tried to call. Instantly she squelched the reaction. After all, she was about to end the relationship, not take it to a more intimate level. "Tuesday night I had dinner with a co-worker, Wednesday I went to a shower for a friend who's having a baby and Thursday...." She wrinkled her nose for a few seconds, trying to recall. "Thursday I worked late."

"Uh-huh. With good-old Walt Gladwin?"

"I explained that he's working very hard to finish up those documents before I leave on my trip," she reminded him quietly.

"All I knew was that you weren't home to answer your phone."

Kelsey swung around and found him studying her far too intently. It occurred to her in that moment that, if she had allowed the affair to commence, she would have found Cole Stockton to be a very possessive man. He must have seen the knowledge in her hazel-green eyes, because he continued to assess her expression for another long moment before nodding once.

"You're right," he told her. "I didn't like it. And I'm going to dislike it more and more. I want to know where you are and what you're doing. And I don't want to have to wonder three nights in a row if you're with another man."

Kelsey found herself reacting to the implied threat almost without thinking. "Don't worry. You won't have to concern yourself with that problem ever again."

A speculative gleam lit Cole's gray eyes. "Is that a promise?"

"I'm afraid so," Kelsey said wearily. She avoided his pinning gaze and walked across the room, feeling an urgent need to put some distance between herself and this man. She came to a halt in front of the fire that blazed in the black granite fireplace. Cole had kindled the flames just before they had sat down to the dinner of cracked crab and salad they'd prepared together.

"Kelsey, what are you trying to say, honey?" he asked softly.

"You missed the whole point of that little story I told you a few minutes ago, Cole," she said, gazing down into the flames. "The lesson I learned from that disaster two years ago was not that long-distance relations are difficult, but rather that any good relationship must be built on trust and honesty. I need to know that the man who's asking a commitment of me is being totally upfront and aboveboard. I don't want any hidden barriers, any secrets or any nasty surprises."

"Hell, I'm not hiding a wife and six kids somewhere," he told her with a flash of rare humor. "Word of honor." He held up one hand, palm out.

Kelsey looked up, refusing to respond to his attempt at lightness. "But I can't be certain of that, can I? I can't be certain of anything at all about you or your life before you moved to Carmel. You're a closed book to me, Cole. A locked chest. You refuse to discuss your past, you won't tell me anything except the most elementary facts about yourself. You don't seem to care about the future. You deal only in the present. There's no way I can really get to know you."

"Kelsey," he began harshly, "that's enough. I realize you're a little tense tonight and that you've had a hard week, but—"

"Cole, listen to me. I am not tense because of my hard workweek. I'm tense because I'm trying to find a polite way of telling you I'm not going to see you again. One solid month of trying to establish some kind of toehold in that wall you've built around yourself is enough for me. Our relationship, long distance or otherwise, is going nowhere fast, and I intend to end it before it becomes destructive."

Raw power and cold masculine fury crackled to life in the beautiful room with the force of an exploding incendiary grenade. Kelsey barely had time to assimilate the knowledge that she'd handled everything all wrong when the sound of splintering glass filled the air.

She watched, stunned, as the brandy snifter Cole had been holding seemed to disintegrate between his fingers. For an electric instant both she and Cole stared at the shards of glass as they dropped to the floor. Her mother's fine crystal had dissolved under the crushing force of his hand.

Cole snapped out of the frozen, charged silence that had gripped the room. "Don't even think of trying to run. You wouldn't make it through the door."

TWO

"Cole, stop it! You don't understand."

"I understand." Cole felt the anger and the hot desire flooding through him, a potent combination unlike anything he had ever experienced. "I understand everything. Did you think you could play games with me for a month and then walk out?"

"I wasn't playing games."

He watched her back away from him, one hand held out in front of her as if she could placate him or ward him off. He moved toward her with a cool stride, willing her to realize how inevitable the outcome of this confrontation was going to be for both of them.

"For a month we've been doing this your way," he said roughly. "I told myself I wouldn't rush you, that I'd give you all the time you needed. I wanted you to feel comfortable with me."

"'Comfortable'! How can I feel comfortable with a man who refuses to tell me anything important about himself?" she flung back. Still trying to maintain a distance between them, Kelsey was working her way steadily toward the sliding-glass doors at the other end of the room.

"I've answered your damn questions," Cole gritted. "We've had all kinds of long conversations. You seemed to like them so much that I've spent just about every weekend talking to you until two in the morning!"

"But you never tell me anything," she wailed.

"The hell I don't! I've told you everything you needed to know. Everything that affects our lives. You know where I live, what I do for a living, how I feel about the state of the economy, politics, Thai food and saving whales."

"But whenever I ask about your past you refuse to answer."

"That's because my past is not important to either of us," he informed her with cold arrogance. "It has no bearing on our relationship. Who do you think you are to demand explanations and answers just to satisfy your feminine curiosity? I have never lied to you and I never will lie to you. That's all you need to know. If there are matters I prefer not to discuss, you can take it they aren't important."

He saw the fury that sizzled in her near-green eyes and watched it do battle with the very female fear he had inspired. He wanted to see the wariness and uncertainty in her tonight because it meant that at last she was finally taking him seriously. But a part of him respected the anger and defiance, too. He had known from the beginning that he wanted Kelsey Murdock, and her pride was part of the package. Cole had promised himself he would handle that streak of pride and independence carefully. Until tonight he'd done a fairly good job, he thought.

"How can you claim your past isn't important?" she challenged, backing another step. "You could be a...a gangster or an international jewel thief. For all I know you could have been living here in Carmel under an assumed name for the past year. Maybe you're a syndicate hit man who only has to do a couple of big jobs a year and has the rest of the time to live in luxury. If you call living behind iron gates and high stone walls a luxurious manner of living, that is!"

"You've really let your imagination run wild, haven't you? I had no idea you were spinning such fantasies."

"What kind of fantasies did you expect me to dream up about your past when you won't tell me anything about it?"

"I expect you to ignore my past, not sit around making up fairy tales."

"You seem interested enough in what I've been doing for the past twenty-eight years," she retorted vengefully.

"Only because you've been willing to talk about it. If you hadn't wanted to discuss it, I would have respected that."

"I'm willing to talk about it because I have nothing to hide!"

"Implying I do? Forget it, Kelsey, you're not going to goad me into making any interesting confessions. If there were anything I thought you should know, I'd tell you."

She came to the sliding-glass doors and found herself forced to halt. Defiantly she lifted her head, and the recessed ceiling light fell on her taut features.

Kelsey was not a beautiful woman, but the lively intelligence in her eyes and the promise of tenderness and passion in her warm smile had tugged at Cole since the moment he'd met her. Technically, she probably only qualified as reasonably attractive. Emotionally, she drew him to her with a heady combination of factors. Kelsey could be charming and witty or soft and reflective. She could be gentle and perceptive or aggressive and teasing. The fundamental sensuality in her seemed to have been designed specifically to attract him. Even the scent of her was unique and intoxicating. In short, she had a power over Cole he couldn't fully explain but that he acknowledged completely.

What she didn't realize, apparently, he told himself ruthlessly, was that he had power over her, too. Or he intended to institute it. It was time she understood that.

"I'm not going to continue in a relationship that's conducted one hundred percent by your rules, Cole. I'll make my own decisions about what I think is important and what I should know."

"Arrogant little witch," he breathed, not without a hint of admiration. "Do you think you can just call off our affair because I refuse to satisfy every aspect of your curiosity?"

"Yes," she declared vehemently. "I do. I can call it off for whatever reason pleases me. Actually, to be perfectly factual about this association of ours, I don't think you can call it a relationship, let alone an affair."

"Because I've only kissed you good-night a few

times? Because I've let you send me home to a lonely bed every night we've been together? Lady, if you think that means we haven't started an affair, you're deluding yourself. I wanted to give you time, damn it!"

"Why? So that I could get to know you better?" she asked scathingly. "That's a joke, considering your attitude toward questions!"

"I've been wasting my time, haven't I?" Cole drawled, halting a few feet away to study her. She was poised to make a frantic dash out through the sliding-glass door, he realized. Her fingers were hovering on the handle.

"I think I'm the one who's been wasting time," Kelsey told him evenly. "But perhaps you're right. Perhaps we're both making the same mistake. We're obviously not right for each other, Cole. I think that when you've had a chance to think about it you'll realize that. You need some mindless little powder puff who won't want a relationship that goes any farther than the bedroom."

"And what do you need, Kelsey?" he asked deliberately, watching her hand without appearing to do so. Her fingers were tightening around the door handle now. In another moment she would yank open the door and make a dash for it. He wondered almost idly where she thought she could run to that he wouldn't find her. Perhaps he'd let her flee for a short distance out into the misty night. It might teach her a lesson. A rain-soaked woman trying to run across a sandy beach while wearing a pair of ridiculously high heels would soon sense her own vulnerability.

"I need a man who can share all of himself—past,

present and future. A man who believes in honest relationships. I also need someone who's in tune enough with me and the modern world to know that the last thing he should offer is to make me his paid mistress!"

With that she made her bid for escape. Cole watched with almost lazy indulgence as she flung open the sliding door and darted out onto the wide veranda that overlooked the beach. She turned anxiously to glance back at him before starting down the steps that led to the beach.

"Where are you going to go, Kelsey?" he asked softly as she stood tensed for flight. "My home is about the nearest source of refuge. It's a long walk into Carmel. And it's very wet and cold out there tonight, isn't it?"

He watched the effect of his words as she stood under the veranda light. The fury and the fear were still engaged in a fierce tug-of-war in her eyes.

"Why are you trying to terrify me, Cole? Just to get even for the fact that I've decided not to let you seduce me?"

"I'm not trying to terrify you. I'm going to make love to you. It's what I've been planning to do all evening and I'm not about to change my mind now."

Deliberately he stepped through the sliding-glass door, and her nerve broke. Kelsey turned and ran down the steps, out into the misty rain. Sighing at the prospect of having to get wet, Cole went after her. He was in no rush. She couldn't possibly run far in those shoes. Soon she would realize the hopelessness of trying to flee, and the psychological impact of that realization would be useful.

Besides, he reminded himself bleakly, this wasn't the first time he'd set an ambush in the rain.

It wasn't hard keeping her in sight. The fiery-red knit dress was a light, shifting patch of muted color against the darkness, and the pale skin of her legs provided an equally visible target.

Cole knew, without bothering to think about it, that in his black pullover and slacks he was probably already invisible to her. He watched her turn to the left as she hit the beach and saw her stumble a little on the damp, packed sand. She glanced back again to see if he was following. Standing near the twisted trunk of a Monterey cypress, Cole smiled grimly to himself. She couldn't see him at all now. That much was obvious. He saw her hesitate, trying to search the darkness. But fading into nearby cover was a skill that came so naturally to Cole he knew she couldn't possibly detect his presence.

Out on the beach, Kelsey tried desperately to assess the situation. It had been idiotic to allow him to frighten her into running outside. Running wasn't even possible in the high heels she was wearing, she had discovered. There was no sign of him as she glanced back toward the house, but the chilly, drizzling rain had already begun to soak the red knit dress and dampen her hair. She felt ridiculous.

To top it off, she'd let him chase her out of her own home, she thought furiously. Well, her parents' home. Same difference. He belonged in that walled fortress up the beach, not in her mother's beautiful, airy house. Kelsey wondered dismally how long he'd wait for her to come back.

Kelsey stood, miserable and wet, her heels sunk into the sand, and stared longingly back at the warmly lit house. Inside was a fire on the hearth, a hot shower and a glass of brandy waiting.

There was also Cole.

He had shocked her with his violent reaction to her decision to end the relationship. It had been stunningly clear that he'd planned to take her to bed tonight, and he hadn't liked her throwing his intentions off stride. She'd guessed he wouldn't like the rejection, but she hadn't been prepared for the fury it had elicited.

There was no movement on the veranda and none in the shadows that filtered through the misty rain. Behind her the surf tossed noisily, making it impossible to hear any other minor sounds. Not that Cole would make so much as a whisper when he moved, Kelsey thought nervously. A tangled cypress tree loomed in front of her as she stepped uncertainly back toward the shelter of her mother's home.

She couldn't continue to stand out here in the rain like a soggy terrier. Besides, she was very cold now. There was nothing to fear from Cole, not really, she told herself optimistically. After all, he was her parents' neighbor and friend. Surely he wouldn't risk incurring their wrath by assaulting her, she assured herself. It had been silly to allow him to intimidate her into running.

It was just that she knew so little about Cole Stockton. She couldn't really be sure of anything, including the notion that he might not resort to genuine violence.

She took another step closer to the house, drawn toward it now as a means of escape from the steady discomfort of the rain. Her own anger and the feeling of having been made to act idiotically fed her increasingly positive view of the situation. So what if Cole was still waiting for her inside, she asked herself. She could handle him. She'd call his bluff and tell him exactly where he could go.

Kelsey was bracing herself with that last thought when Cole's hand settled tightly around her wrist. She opened her mouth instinctively to scream and promptly felt his palm across her lips as he materialized from the shadow of the cypress.

"It's not that I'm afraid anyone will actually hear you and come to your rescue," he rasped softly. "It's just that I'd like to protect my own ears."

She panicked as she sensed the inescapable quality of his hold. All thoughts of being able to handle him faded. Frantically she tried to struggle, beating at Cole with her free hand until he somehow managed to lock it between their bodies. The strength of him was overwhelming. He wielded it with a casual ease that told her precisely how little her efforts mattered.

When she managed to get in one good kick that caught his leg a solid blow, Cole abruptly turned impatient. Binding her to him so that she was crushed against his chest, he captured her face and brought his mouth close to hers.

"Did you think you could run from me tonight?" he asked against her lips as the rain fell gently. "I've been waiting for you for a whole month. I know you want me as much as I want you, so sheathe your claws, Kelsey. Tonight you're going to find out what's really important between us."

Kelsey grabbed for her courage. "Let me go, you bastard. I've had enough of your way of conducting a 'relationship.' I'll bet you actually do have something to hide, don't you? An honest man, a man with any sensitivity wouldn't dream of behaving like this!"

She got no further, because he was driving the abusive words back into her throat with the force of his kiss. Kelsey tasted the rain on his mouth, and then he was inside her own. There was a savage possession in his kiss that she sensed could only be satisfied with her complete surrender. She could feel the demand in every part of her body.

For a month she had been tantalizing herself with fantasies of what it would be like to make love with Cole. Until now she knew the few kisses she had received had been carefully restrained, designed to warm the fires of attraction that flared between them but not intending to set them ablaze. Cole had been biding his time, she realized dimly. He had hidden the full extent of his passion from her with a self-restraint that was incredible.

Kelsey had sensed she would find excitement and fire in his arms, but she had not guessed at the depths of the desire that would flame within her when Cole released himself from the barriers he had established. The chilled rain was forgotten under the intensity of his kiss. His arms were locked around Kelsey with such force that she knew she could not escape. His tongue swept into the farthest recesses of her mouth, taunting, daring, conquering, until she went limp against him.

"What made you think you could end everything

we've started just because you weren't getting some answers to your foolish question?" he grated as he dragged his mouth damply away from hers.

Kelsey could only stare up at his face, stricken with the knowledge of just how helpless she was. A part of her longed fiercely to surrender to the passion he ignited, but another part of her rebelled at the way it was all happening. She had made her decision before leaving San Jose, she tried to remind herself. It had been the right one—she was sure of it. At least she had been sure of it in the cold light of day. But tonight...

"You have no right to force me into bed with you," she bit out desperately.

"'No right'? When I can make you tremble like this just by kissing you? You're the one who's so gung ho for truth and honesty, Kelsey. Why don't you admit you want me? I've seen it in your eyes. I've felt it in your touch. You're only resisting now because you're so independent and stubborn. I told you earlier this evening that you are going to have to learn to make some compromises in this affair, and I'm going to start teaching you the meaning of the word tonight."

"Cole, no! Put me down," she objected as he swung her into his arms and started back toward the house.

"I'll make love to you in the rain on some other occasion, Kelsey. It's too damn cold out here tonight. We need a hot shower and a warm bed."

"That isn't what I want." Her nails sank into the wet fabric of his pullover.

"It's what you want, all right. It just isn't happening quite the way you wanted it to happen. I would have done things your way, Kelsey, if you hadn't thrown down the gauntlet tonight." He was on the steps leading up to the veranda now. "I would have given you all the time you wanted, within reason. But you had to push a little too hard, didn't you? You have a lot to learn."

"I refuse to begin an affair with a man I can't trust," she flared.

"Tell me you still refuse and that you don't trust me after we've spent the night together," he challenged tightly. "By morning the world is going to look very different to you, Kelsey. I'll see to that."

"One night in bed with you isn't going to change anything," she protested wildly as he carried her inside the house.

"Tell me that in the morning," he taunted. Cole balanced her easily as he slammed the sliding-glass door shut. Then he started down the hall to the bedroom that Kelsey used when she stayed in her mother's home.

Torn between panic and desire, Kelsey caught her breath and began to struggle again as Cole walked into the cream-and-yellow bedroom. "You can't do this to me and you know it. I don't care what kind of attitude you've got toward the rights of others, you can't treat me like this!"

His cool gray gaze swept over her as he stood her on her feet. "I'm an old friend of the family's, remember. All I'm going to do is take care of you, see that you get properly warmed after that stupid dash out into the rain."

"Cole, listen to me," she pleaded, her voice wavering under the impact of his relentlessness. "We need to talk. Communicate. That's what's been wrong with this...this relationship of ours since the beginning. You keep drawing lines and putting up walls. You haven't let me get to know you."

His fingers went to the first of the gold buttons on her red dress. "You'll know everything you need to know by morning."

"Damn you, I won't let you do this to me!" Tears of frustration and rage burned in her eyes as Kelsey tried to slap aside his hands. She was cold and wet and miserable. She was also more than a little frightened. She knew she was dealing with a man and a situation that had, in a matter of minutes, flared out of her control. And the most shattering aspect of the matter was that she was no longer in full control of herself, either.

"Stop fighting me, Kelsey," Cole urged huskily as he caught her wrists and pinned them quite gently behind her back. "I'm doing this for your sake, as well as mine."

"At least spare me the self-righteous act."

"Look at me, Kelsey," he ordered softly, using his free hand to lift her chin. "Look at me and tell me you don't want me."

"I don't want—" she began heatedly, only to have the words cut off as he stopped them with a warning kiss. Kelsey's mind and body absorbed the threat along with the heavy passion behind it. Every inch of her was tingling with awareness and longing. She could no more stop her response to this man than she could stop the rain in the night.

"The truth, Kelsey. Give me that much at least."

"Why should I?" she breathed painfully. "You won't give me the same in return."

"You've always had the truth from me. You always will," he vowed. "I may not tell you everything you want to know, but what I do choose to tell you is for real."

"That's not good enough!" she cried.

"It's going to have to be good enough." Once more he kissed her, crushing her against the length of his body until she could feel the hard planes and angles of him through his damp clothing. When he lifted his head this time there was raw, insistent demand in his bluntly hewn features. "Admit you've wanted me this past month. Tell me you've known from the beginning that sooner or later we would find ourselves in bed together."

"There was nothing inevitable about it," she said shakily, and knew now that she lied. It was shockingly, brilliantly clear to her senses that this moment had been preordained from the first time she had met Cole Stockton. Why was she trying to deny herself this night, she wondered.

"Kelsey, Kelsey," he murmured huskily. "I can feel you trembling in my arms. Don't lie to me, honey." He drew his hand down the line of her vulnerable throat and once more found the gold buttons of the red knit dress. This time he undid them methodically, each action a caress. By the time he had finished, Kelsey was leaning helplessly into his strength, tiny tremors of desire racing through her, sapping her will. When Cole finally slipped his hand deliberately inside the parted material of the dress and found her breast she had to swallow her instinctive cry of longing.

"Oh, Cole..."

"I can feel what you're trying to tell me, sweetheart. Just relax and let it all happen as it was meant to happen." He allowed her to bury her face against the fabric of his sweater as if he knew she would find it easier that way.

"Cole, this won't change anything," Kelsey managed, but her voice was thick with emotion. "In the morning..."

"I'm not interested in anything but the present. We'll worry about tonight now. The morning will take care of itself." He stroked the dusky rose tip of her small breast with the pad of his thumb. "Your nipples are like hard little berries, Kelsey. Earlier this evening I could see their outline through your dress and I knew you hadn't worn a bra. You wanted me to know, didn't you? It was an invitation. A small act of intimacy. And it made my head spin just thinking of what it meant."

"Cole," she said, sighing. "You don't understand." But in a way she knew he did. He certainly understood the depths of the physical attraction between them. And he seemed to comprehend completely just how thoroughly he could dominate her senses.

"Hush, Kelsey," he soothed, lowering his head to kiss the sensitive skin just under her ear. His fingers toyed with the damp strands of her hair. "I'm not going to wait any longer for you." He paused, letting the tip of his thumb graze her flowering nipple again. "Want me, Kelsey?"

She shuddered, giving up the pointless battle. "I

want you, Cole. But it won't change anything in the morning."

"For our purposes tonight the future is as nonexistent as the past." Then he covered her mouth with his own, holding it captive, while he stripped the red knit dress from her body.

In one mind-shattering moment, Kelsey found herself naked in front of him, shivering from the cold of the rain and the heat of desire. He freed her hands and she moaned gently, wrapping her arms around his neck.

"Kelsey, I've wanted to see you like this for so long." Cole's palms slicked down her sides, following the contours of waist and thigh with a hungry touch. She heard the deep groan in his chest. "Come on, honey. We need a hot shower. We're both too cold and wet."

He led her into the bathroom, tossing aside his sweater and stepping out of his shoes and slacks with impatient efficiency. Kelsey was unable to take her eyes from the strong, lean body, revealed as he undressed. When he reached out to shove aside the yellow shower curtain and turn on the water, the muscles of his broad shoulders moved with smooth coordination.

Cole turned to confront her as the shower came on, and Kelsey felt a rush of nervous anticipation as she saw the full extent of his arousal. He smiled one of his very rare smiles as he took in the expression in her eyes.

"Come here, Kelsey. You know as well as I do that there's no turning back now." He held out his hand.

After the briefest of hesitations, Kelsey put her fingers in his and allowed him to tug her under the hot spray. The water chased away the shivers that had been caused by the cold rain but not the tremors of rising passion. They only seemed to increase.

"You're so sleek and soft, Kelsey," Cole whispered into her wet hair as he pulled her against him. "Feel what you do to me."

"I've already seen what I do to you," she blurted out unthinkingly, and then flushed at the passionate amusement in his eyes. "I mean—"

"I couldn't possibly hide my reaction to you. Why should I?" He accepted his body's fierce arousal with arrogant complacency. "But I want you to feel it, not just see it."

He captured her wrists and drew her hands down his chest. Kelsey stared in fascination as her wine-tinted nails trailed through the crisp hair that tapered down to his flat stomach. She found herself flexing her fingers just to feel the taut hardness beneath his skin.

"Little cat," he muttered, and then he forced her hands even lower.

"Do you really want me so badly?" she heard herself ask tremulously, a strange sensation of feminine power springing to life in her.

"I think I'd lose my mind tonight if I didn't take you." He released her wrists and cupped her breasts, bending down to nip at the exquisitely sensitized tips with teasing hunger.

Kelsey shuddered delicately as he reached around her waist to grasp her hips. She felt him drawing her tightly into the hardness of his lower body.

"My God, lady. What made you think I'd let you

walk away from me tonight?" He began to probe gently between the softness of her thighs, his fingers searching and finding the part of her that was dampening of its own accord, not because of the shower. "And what," he added meaningfully as he felt the slick evidence of her longing, "made you think you could deny either of us?"

She didn't answer. There was no point trying to deal with the complex emotions storming through her, at least not on an intellectual basis. Right at this moment Kelsey could only feel and respond. Everything tonight was beyond anything she had ever experienced. For a month she had been tormenting herself with fantasies and dreams, all of which she had decided must not be fulfilled. But if she had been able to estimate even a fraction of what the real thing with Cole would be like she would have known the decision was out of her hands.

Slowly, with an intensity that left her shaking, Cole explored her body. In harsh, heavy whispers he urged her to return the intimate favor. At the mercy of the unfamiliar passion and need, Kelsey obeyed. She touched him with every emotion from delight and shyness to tenderness and aggression.

Cole welcomed all her myriad responses, clearly glorying in her uncontrollable reactions. Under his hands she drifted further and further into the whirling vortex of his desire and was barely aware of the moment when he turned off the shower. She was vividly conscious of her rising impatience as he insisted on towel-drying her hair and her body, however. When he had finished the task she was flushed and tingling with need.

"Please, Cole," she pleaded, clinging to him as he quickly dried himself.

"I told you," he reminded her thickly, "I told you that in the end you'd be begging me."

Later she would remember both the words and the satisfaction in his voice, but right now they were unimportant. "I want you," she admitted almost violently.

"And I want you. Believe me, I want you more than anything else on the face of the earth." He picked her up again, striding back into the darkened bedroom. There he settled her in the middle of the turned-back bed, coming down beside her with a dark growl of desire.

Cole gathered Kelsey to him, heating her body with his own, inflaming her with ancient words and even more primitive caresses. Kelsey was a shivering, demanding, uninhibited female creature by the time he rose above her.

"Now, sweetheart. It has to be now. I can't wait another moment for you. Open yourself, Kelsey. I'm going to make you mine."

Something in his words got through to her; perhaps the grim promise in them when instinctively Kelsey knew she should be hearing a passionate plea. Whatever it was, combined with the bold, aggressive manner in which he parted her legs and lowered himself to her, it caused her to surface briefly. A sensation of real danger and a vague realization of the incredible emotional risk she was taking made Kelsey stiffen in belated resistance.

"No, Kelsey. It was all over for you weeks ago," Cole rasped as he felt the sudden tensing of her body. Deliberately he moved his hand to her thighs, stroking the throbbingly sensitive bud of passion hidden there.

Kelsey cried out, her nails digging into the skin of his shoulders. Her head arched back in invitation as she lifted her lower body against his hand.

"See, honey?" he groaned. "It's much too late." He fitted himself to her soft, warm opening and before she could summon any further protest he thrust deeply. "Ah, Kelsey, Kelsey...."

Her body accepted the invasion and Kelsey gave herself up to the shimmering excitement, thrilling to the crushing weight of the man who held her so tightly. He set the pace of the lovemaking, dominating the rhythm as if intent on imprinting her body with his own. Every small moan in the back of her throat, every pleading arch of her hips, every urgent demand of her hands he took with passion and satisfaction.

Kelsey felt filled, her body stretched deliciously tight until each nerve ending threatened to explode. On and on the heavy, thrusting rhythm went, driving her higher and higher up a spiral staircase of need. She had never climbed to such heights, never seen the highest steps with any man. Tonight the rapidity with which she gained the top was dazzling.

"Cole, oh, my God, Cole...!"

"Hang on to me, Kelsey. Just hang on to me. I'll take care of you...."

And then they were both crying out each other's

names, over and over again as the pulsing completion spun them away from the last vestiges of reality.

Cole felt himself recovering slowly, a sensation of infinity coalescing around him. It took him a moment or two to realize that the soft, exciting gasps of the woman under him had become long, relaxed breaths. Kelsey's lashes fluttered restlessly and then lifted. He found himself gazing down into the bottomless depths of her eyes. In the shadowy light of the bedroom he could not begin to read the mixture of emotions swirling there.

"Kelsey?" he whispered as he reluctantly unsealed their bodies. "Are you all right?" He settled down beside her, cradling her in the crook of his arm.

"Yes."

He smiled. "You scared me there for a moment. You looked somewhat shell-shocked."

"Yes."

His faint smile disappeared as he watched her close her eyes again. Damn it, what was she thinking, he wondered, experiencing the first touch of uncertainty he'd had all evening. He'd felt the total response of her body, heard the words of desire on her lips. And he knew beyond a shadow of a doubt that he'd given her complete satisfaction. So why was she closing her eyes and trying to shut him out?

Because he had the distinct impression that was exactly what she was doing. Uneasily he stirred beside her, tangling his legs with hers. She didn't resist the small intimacy, but neither did she open her eyes.

"Kelsey, where the hell do you think you're going?" he demanded as he realized she was drifting away from him, trying to isolate herself.

"Is it all right if I go to sleep, Cole?" she asked with a suspicious meekness.

"Kelsey, I want to talk to you."

"You said we'd talk in the morning."

Cole stifled an impatient sigh and reached out to smooth the tendrils of her tawny hair off her cheek. He knew he was growing angry and knew, too, that it was a ridiculous reaction on his part.

He'd achieved his goal, he reminded himself. After tonight Kelsey would never be able to deny the passion they generated in each other. And, he told himself forcefully, she wouldn't be able to pretend she was free any longer. He knew by the way she had responded tonight he could repeat the experience anytime he wished. She was his on a very fundamental level. No matter what she tried to tell herself intellectually, he only had to reach out and take her in order to remind her of the bonds he had put in place.

But somehow all the conviction in the world wasn't countering the growing uneasiness in his gut. He'd pushed her hard tonight, Cole admitted as he stared up at the ceiling. He'd lost his control when she'd startled him by saying she was going to end the relationship. Of all the words he had expected from her tonight, those were the last he'd thought he would hear.

He'd been furious that she could even think of withdrawing. And, if the truth be told, he acknowledged, he'd felt the cutting edge of something close to panic.

Panic was an alien reaction for Cole Stockton. The necessity of surviving under deadly conditions had taught him self-control a long time ago. It had taken

Kelsey Murdock to introduce him to the recklessness and panic only true desperation could produce.

He'd had no choice tonight, Cole decided grimly. It was a case of either acting forcefully or running the risk of having Kelsey walk out.

But he'd really pushed her, another part of his mind reminded him. She was going to have some adjustments to make in the morning. He should allow her some time now to come to terms with herself and with him.

Cole turned his head on the pillow and saw that Kelsey had gone to sleep. Initially he'd planned on spending the night in her bed, but now he asked himself if he shouldn't provide her with some breathing space.

He'd like to be here in the morning. It would be very pleasant to make long, slow love to her at dawn. Then they could fix breakfast together and spend the rest of the day talking about their relationship....

But perhaps that schedule, satisfying though it would be for him, wouldn't give her the private time she might need to deal with what had happened. He realized now that he wasn't quite certain what to do next.

Uncertainty was almost as alien to him as panic, Cole thought with a grimace. Kelsey was teaching him a great deal tonight, and he didn't particularly appreciate the lessons. On the other hand, he assured himself, rising carefully from the bed, he'd taught her a crucial lesson, too.

He stood for a long moment, looking down at her curved body, and then he reached to draw the quilt up over her shoulders. He was tempted to crawl back under that quilt with her. In the end he resisted.

He'd been stalking his quarry for a month now, and tonight he'd been forced to close the trap far more aggressively than he'd ever anticipated. The hunter in him sensed that he should back off a bit and allow Kelsey time to accept what had happened.

At least Cole thought it was his hunting instincts that issued the advice. A cold prickle of wariness warned him it might be the strange new element of uncertainty guiding his actions. Or the panic. He could no longer be sure.

Retrieving his still-damp clothing, Cole dressed and prepared to leave the bedroom. He hesitated a moment in the doorway, feeling the invisible pull of the sleeping woman. She had been everything he had dreamed or imagined she would be in his arms—passionate, exciting, soft and captivating. He had to work at summoning the self-discipline he needed to leave the room. But Cole had a lot of experience calling on self-discipline.

He walked down the hall and stepped out into the night, disappearing into the shadows and the misty rain as if he were a natural part of the darkness around him.

THREE

Kelsey awoke early the next morning, struggling upright in bed with a gnawing sense of doom. Memories of the night flooded back. Nothing had gone right. Nothing had gone as she had planned. The small twinges she felt in her thighs as she pushed back the covers and got to her feet reinforced the knowledge that she had fouled up very badly. She must have been a fool to assume she could handle Cole Stockton in a straightforward, honest, civilized manner.

She had sensed he could be dangerous, Kelsey reminded herself as she padded wearily into the bathroom. But she hadn't realized just how completely he lived by his own rules. And if she was honest with herself she had to acknowledge she hadn't dreamed just how primitive her own responses could be under such circumstances.

Last night. She couldn't quite believe what had happened last night.

She must have gone crazy, Kelsey thought as she sought refuge in the shower. She should have fought Cole, threatened to call the police, screamed rape. Instead she had allowed herself to be whirled away on a tide of passion unlike anything she had ever known. It had all seemed so inevitable, so irresistible last night. He had pursued her, captured her and claimed her, and she had accepted his right to do so. On some fundamental level she had accepted him.

Kelsey closed her eyes in anguished memory. Never had she been so much at the mercy of her own desire, let alone the mercy of a man. It was almost impossible to comprehend her actions.

Where had it all gone wrong, she questioned time and again as she went through the ritual of showering and dressing. She had known that every weekend in Carmel was becoming increasingly risky. She had realized the attraction between her and Cole was a smoldering fire that could easily singe her fingers if she wasn't careful. Well, last night she had not been careful enough, and more than her fingers had been burned. Kelsey felt as if her whole body had gone up in flames.

He had been so furious when she'd tried to tell him she wouldn't see him again. Accustomed to his controlled, quiet responses to almost any situation, Kelsey simply hadn't been prepared for the sudden blazing power that had erupted in him. In her mind she would see that shattered brandy glass for a long time to come.

Kelsey winced as she pulled on gray pleated trousers and a long-sleeved persimmon sweater. Her body was going to be a long time forgetting last night, too. Cole had been a demanding, overwhelming lover. He had gone about eliciting her responses with a bold aggressive passion that had been captivating.

Angrily Kelsey tugged on low suede boots and

stalked out into the living room. Passion, physical attraction, *sex*. That's all it could have amounted to, given the fact there was no basis for any genuine relationship between Cole Stockton and her.

He had steadfastly refused to allow her close in any meaningful way. He had refused to confide in her, or let her get to know anything about the forces that had shaped his life. He wouldn't answer questions about his past, and he arrogantly assured her she had no need to know the answers.

And in addition to all his other sins, she decided furiously, the man hadn't even stayed through the night. He'd walked out right after seducing her.

Not that there was any reason he should have remained, Kelsey told herself bitterly as she poured dry cereal into a bowl and located a carton of milk. He got what he wanted, didn't he? He had his revenge. He'd made a mockery of her cool decision to end the relationship. Then he'd calmly walked out.

Kelsey sat tensely on the stool in front of the marble counter, her booted feet hooked over the bottom rung. She munched cereal while she waited for the coffee to make itself in the drip machine, and she thought about her own foolishness at great length.

It wasn't until she was on her second cup of strong coffee that her basic spirit began to revive. Every woman made a few mistakes in her life when it came to dealing with the male of the species.

"So why can't I calmly sit here and write off last night as a bad error in judgment?" she said aloud.

It just wasn't going to be that easy. Picking up the mug of coffee, Kelsey wandered into the living room, noting gloomily that the rain had stopped. She must have been crazy to make that dash outside last night. No, she hadn't been nuts. She'd been scared. Panicked by a man at her age. Well, with good reason, as it turned out, she thought with a sigh.

Unfortunately that sense of panic had not completely vanished. A part of her insisted on feeling that something elemental had changed in her life and she wasn't going to escape the consequences.

One thing was certain. She couldn't stay here this weekend. Not when Cole Stockton lived virtually next door. The thought of running into him in Carmel or during a walk on the beach sent real shivers down her spine. Her instincts this morning were to go into hiding, she realized wryly.

Absently she began to water her mother's plants. The little task was, after all, supposed to be her chief excuse for coming down to Carmel each weekend during the past month. She would carry it out as usual this morning, and then she would run.

Promising herself the escape did not lighten Kelsey's feeling of tension. It was as if deep down she knew that running away this morning wasn't going to do any more good than running away last night had done. But she forced herself to concentrate on getting away from Cole Stockton as she walked through the house with the brass watering pot.

In her stepfather's study she paused to look at the sleek home computer she had helped him select a few months ago. Roger Evans had been as delighted with his new toy as any child. He had a passion for order and precision when it came to maintaining his personal financial records and the computer was a perfect mechanism for providing this. With the expertise she had naturally picked up working at Flex-Glad, Kelsey had been able to give her stepfather a lot of advice and assistance. She had even presented him with a copy of the new, very sophisticated accounting program Flex-Glad had recently perfected.

Working together on the project had established a firm friendship between Roger and her. Kelsey had been quite pleased at her mother's decision to remarry, and she had found Roger to be charming from the first. But it wasn't until she had helped him choose his computer and had taught him how to use the accounting program that she had really had a chance to get to know Roger Evans.

Impulsively she sat down in front of the terminal. She was curious to find out how far her stepfather had gone with the accounting potential of the new Flex-Glad program. With the computer warmed up, she shoved the correct diskette into the drive and called up the list of files she and Roger had established.

IRS
JOURNAL
GEN LEDG
A.E. INV

That last file was the one in which Roger tracked her mother's investments. There wasn't much either of them could do about the decisions regarding the administration of the money, as it was all in the hands of the bank, but Roger loved to keep up with the bank's choices all the same. He simply thrived on the intricacies of orderly accounting procedures. It was much more than a hobby.

"You should have been an accountant," Kelsey had told him once.

"Probably should have been," Roger had replied with a chuckle. "But I came from a family of lawyers, and there was never much choice about my career, I'm afraid. It was either law or utter disgrace."

"Ah, the perils of being born into East Coast preppydom," Kelsey had teased affectionately.

Roger had agreed with a surprising degree of seriousness. "One's background can place a great many limitations on one. There are times when it would be very pleasant to simply close the door behind yourself in life and open a new one. But it takes courage. A lot of it."

Kelsey thought about that conversation now, wondering if that was exactly what Cole Stockton had done. Perhaps he had closed a door behind himself and started over.

Bringing with him the money he'd made in his other life, she reminded herself firmly. Mustn't forget that little fact. What kind of life could it have been that it had provided him with so much money he could now afford to sit back and simply manage his investments? Or perhaps, as she had speculated last night, his other life still called to him occasionally. For all she knew, he really could be a very high-priced hit man.

"No more questions about Cole Stockton," she advised herself aloud as she idly glanced down Roger's list of files. "Didn't you learn your lesson last night?"

Why was it that after the trauma of last night she found herself more curious than ever about Cole, she wondered unhappily. Roger, she was pleased to see, had become very creative. In addition to the initial financial record files she had helped him establish there were a few new ones.

EC. IND.
5 YR
STOCK

That first one was probably short for something like "Economic Indicators." The second probably stood for "Five-Year Trends." Roger had mentioned starting such a file for tracking the vagaries of the stock market. And that last file must be another stock-market record. Out of curiosity she called up the actual file in order to see what was inside.

A few seconds later she found herself staring at, first in perplexity and then in shock, the careful notations Roger Evans had entered under the file titled Stock.

The first thing she realized was that "Stock" was not short for a longer file name having to do with tracking the stock market. It was short for Cole Stockton.

The sense of impending doom that had been hovering over her when she awakened intensified by several quantum jumps. She ought to get out of the file right now and shut down the computer. She had no business viewing these records, she told herself. Although up until now Roger had encouraged her to examine what he had been doing with the computer so that she could offer advice, she knew immediately that he would never have intended for her to see this particular file.

There could be no doubt about the type of transaction she was witnessing. Roger was clearly making regular payments to Cole in the amount of a thousand dollars a month.

"My God," Kelsey breathed, staring at the evidence before her eyes. It didn't make sense. *A thousand dollars a month!* Horrifying possibilities danced through her head. Blackmail. A loan. Hush money. She couldn't even guess what else might be included on such a list.

Kelsey's imagination ran wild as she tried to come up with a logical explanation for why Roger should be paying off Cole Stockton. Quickly she backed out of the file and turned off the computer. Then she simply sat staring at the darkened display screen for a very long while.

More questions about Cole Stockton. Always there seemed to be more questions. Never any answers. She remembered the sensation of danger she'd had more than once around the man. Her instincts had been right.

Sudden fury assaulted her, driving her to her feet and out of the study. The brass watering pot sat forgotten beside a small ivy plant as Kelsey stormed out of the room.

It was bad enough that he had invaded her life, demanding that she accept him as a lover without any explanations of his past. It was humiliating that he had offered to set her up as his mistress. It was excruciatingly painful that she would have to live with the fact that he had been able to seduce her so easily.

Damned if she would allow him to intimidate her stepfather on top of everything else!

Snatching up her red calfskin checkbook, Kelsey slammed out of the house. The anger and the hurt of last night fed her recklessness, until she was almost running as she covered the hundred yards separating her mother's home from Cole's fortress.

For the first time since she had met him, Kelsey found herself outside Cole's heavy wrought-iron gate. Viciously she stabbed at the buzzer embedded in the rock wall near the coded lock mechanism.

There was no verbal response through the speaker implanted above the buzzer, but a moment after she had leaned on the button, the front door of the austere white-stucco house opened.

Cole stood in the doorway, watching her intently from across the distance of the neat lawn that ringed his home inside the garden walls. She could not hope to read any nuance of emotion in his face. Cole was a master at concealing his reactions. Except, of course, when he'd lost control last night, Kelsey reminded herself abruptly.

The thought of how he'd become very dangerous very quickly gave her a split second of panic over what she was about to do, but she damped it down under the more fiery anger.

Wrapping her right hand around one of the wrought-iron bars of the gate, she met his eyes. "I've come about the Stockton file," she told him starkly.

Whatever he had been expecting from her, clearly that remark was not it. The cool gray gaze narrowed, and then Cole stepped through the door, starting toward the gate.

He was wearing the familiar neutral khaki slacks and shirt today, and his cordovan brown hair gleamed faintly in the cold sunlight. Kelsey caught her breath as all the remembered intimacy of the night washed over her.

By the time he came to a halt on the opposite side of the huge gate she was having to grab for every ounce of nerve she possessed.

"What in the world are you talking about, Kelsey?" he asked quietly. His hand curled over her fingers as she clenched the iron. When she tried to free herself he tightened the grip, until her fingers were biting into the metal.

"The Stockton file," she repeated evenly. "It's one of Roger's new computer files. And it says he's paying you a thousand dollars a month."

Cole studied her for a long moment before saying very softly, "You've been busy this morning, haven't you? What the hell do you know about that thousand a month?"

"Nothing yet," she snapped. "But I want to know everything. Why is my stepfather paying you that kind of money, Cole?"

He released her to unlatch the heavy gate lock, muttering a short, highly explicit oath as he did so. But his next words were unexpectedly polite. "Have you had breakfast?"

She brushed the question aside impatiently. "Cole, I'm not here to have a pleasant chat over a cup of coffee. I want to know what's going on between you and Roger."

"Come on inside, Kelsey," he instructed. "You may not be in the mood for coffee, but I am." Without waiting to see if she intended to follow, he turned to lead the way toward the house.

Reluctantly, not seeing any other alternative, Kelsey strode after him. Warily she glanced around the walled garden. "Are you expecting a revolution?" she asked caustically. The place reminded her of a military compound.

"It wouldn't be the first," he retorted as he pushed open the heavily paneled front door.

Kelsey stared at his back, astonished. "What's that supposed to mean?"

"Never mind. The breakfast room is this way."

He led her down a tiled hall and through a living room that had been furnished in wicker, wood and bamboo. The serene, almost tropical look surprised Kelsey, and then she reminded herself she hadn't really known what to expect. She hadn't even known enough about Cole to hazard a guess as to the type of environment he would choose for a home. The realization increased her wariness.

The fabulous view of beach and ocean had not been completely sacrificed for the sake of another high stone wall, but it had been impeded somewhat by the tall, wrought-iron grillwork that stood between the house and the beach.

"You have to use a key just to get back and forth to the ocean," she muttered.

"The former owners had the wall built," he told her dismissively.

"I saw the outside of this house a couple of years ago, when the Hendersons lived here. The wall was half its present height in front and there was no wrought-iron fence between the house and the beach."

Cole shrugged as he indicated a wicker chair in the airy breakfast room. "So I made a few modifications."

"You take the phrase 'a man's home is his castle' seriously, don't you?" she scoffed. Kelsey sat down at the glass-topped table, watching as he stepped over to the counter and switched on the coffee machine.

"Kelsey, you didn't come here to make nasty remarks about my home. You've made it clear you don't like the place. Let's move on to another subject."

"The monthly payoffs Roger is making to you?" she suggested boldly. She hadn't cared for the thread of command in his words.

"How about discussing last night, instead?" He leaned back against the counter and pinned her with a brooding expression.

In spite of her determination to remain calm and in control, Kelsey felt the flush that stained her cheeks. "Last night is not on my list of topics open to discussion," she bit back tightly.

"It's about the only one I'm interested in discussing."

His quite resoluteness nearly unnerved her. "You can't expect me to believe that. You're the one who makes it a policy never to rehash the past, remember?"

"That policy applies to my distant past, not the immediate one, and you know it."

"Do you have any idea how incredibly arrogant you are?"

His expression hardened. "I've made a few rules for myself and I live by them. You can call that arrogant if you like—"

"I do."

"I prefer to call it reasonable and prudent. I also call it my prerogative."

Kelsey yanked her eyes from his. Concentrating on the view of the ocean as seen through a row of iron bars, she said, "Forget last night. Any man who truly wanted to discuss last night would have stayed at least until morning." God, she shouldn't have brought that up, she told herself furiously.

There was silence behind her, and then Cole was beside the table where she sat. His movement across the kitchen had been virtually soundless. Kelsey felt his fingers on her chin, lifting her face.

"Is that what this is all about?" he demanded softly. "Are you on the warpath this morning because I didn't stay the whole night?"

"No, damn it, that has nothing to do with the reason I'm here," she protested violently.

He sank down onto the chair next to hers, still cradling her tense face. "Believe me, Kelsey, if I handled that scene all wrong it wasn't intentional. I told myself that you'd need a little time to yourself this morning. I didn't want to push you—"

"You're joking! You didn't want to push me? After you'd already pushed me straight into bed?"

The brackets around his mouth tightened and emotion flickered briefly in the icicle-gray eyes. "You wanted to be there as much as I did."

She flinched, but she was too proud to let her eyes falter. "I will admit I learned something last night, Cole; I found out I'm no more immune to the power of sexual attraction than anyone else."

"Are you going to tell me that's all it was for you?" His thumb moved on her jaw with faint menace. "A bit of sexual adventure?"

"What else could it have been?" she got out flippantly. "Assault?"

"Kelsey, don't push me too hard, okay? When I'm around you I find my self-control isn't quite what it should be," he warned gently.

"I found that out for myself last night."

He shook his head and released her. Silently he got to his feet and went to pour two cups of coffee. "That's about the same time I discovered it, too," he announced dryly. "Along with a few other interesting things."

Kelsey took a grip on her determination. "As I said, I'm not here to discuss last night."

"Ah, yes. You want to know about the thousand a month." Cole carried the mugs of coffee over to the table and sat down again. His attention seemed to be focused entirely on not spilling the coffee, as if a man who moved as smoothly as he did needed to be concerned about such a minor act of coordination. "How did you find out about it, Kelsey?"

She reached for one of the mugs, more out of a desire to find something to do with her suddenly restless hands than because she wanted more coffee. "The records are all neatly stored in Roger's computer," she muttered.

Cole's mouth twisted. "I should have guessed. Roger and his passion for accuracy. Of course he would have entered the information into his new computer." Cole took an experimental sip of his coffee. He gazed thoughtfully out the window now, not looking at Kelsey. "So you went snooping this morning, hmm?"

She stiffened, aware of a lingering sense of guilt. "I wasn't prying. I helped Roger set up those records and I've been into the files a dozen times with him."

"But not that file."

"This file didn't exist the last time I looked at the list in the computer," she gritted.

"And once you saw my name on it, you couldn't resist going into it, right?" Cole appeared half amused and half resigned. "Poor Kelsey. You and your endless questions. You've got the curiosity of a cat, along with a few other feline characteristics, don't you?"

"Cole, I want some answers."

"I know you do. But as usual, you're not going to get them."

She swallowed uncertainly, not liking the blunt finality in his voice. "I mean it, Cole. I want to know what's going on. Why is Roger paying you that money?"

"That's between Roger and me."

"What about my mother?" she demanded.

"Amanda knows nothing about it, either. It doesn't concern her. Furthermore, if you mention the subject to her I'm going to be definitely annoyed," he said mildly.

"Do you honestly expect me to let it drop there? Pretend nothing's going on?"

He gave her a level look. "Nothing *is* going on. At least nothing that concerns you. I've explained that this is entirely between Roger and me."

"Did you loan him money?" Kelsey pressed.

Cole said nothing.

"Are you blackmailing my stepfather?" she asked wildly.

Cole took another sip of his coffee, obviously deliberating his response. "That's a pretty heavy accusation, Kelsey."

"I'm not accusing you. I'm asking you. But you have this policy of not answering questions, don't you?" she reminded him angrily. "A policy of non-communication except when it suits you. How dare you sit there calmly drinking coffee and telling me none of this is my business? If the situation were reversed would you let me tell you to mind your own business? If you thought I was blackmailing a relative of yours would you simply back off and leave the whole matter alone? Hell, I don't even know if you have any relatives!" she concluded in frustrated fury.

"Do you really believe I'm blackmailing Roger?"

"I don't know what to believe. I know virtually nothing about you, thanks to your total failure to communicate!" Lord, she was nearly shouting at him now. Kelsey's fingers trembled around the hand of her coffee mug. It was nerve-racking to lose your temper with a man who was still very much in control of his own.

"We communicated last night, Kelsey."

"That's your idea of communication?" she yelped, leaping to her feet as her emotions threatened to overwhelm her. "You're out of your mind. What in heaven's name made me think we could ever develop a long-term relationship? Forget last night, Cole. It's past history, and we don't talk about past history, remember? I only want to know what you're doing to Roger."

"I'm not doing anything to him."

"Are you blackmailing him?" she demanded.

The gray gaze was as cold as the ocean on a winter's day. "What do you think?"

"That's not an answer!"

He got to his feet with lazy grace, taking a step toward her, which drove Kelsey back against the kitchen wall. "Do you believe I'm blackmailing your stepfather?" Cole lifted his hands, flattening his palms against the wall on either side of her head. There was cool intimidation in every inch of his hard body.

"Cole...."

"Answer me," he ordered.

"I've told you, I don't know what to believe."

"*Answer me.*"

"I don't want to believe it," she gasped.

"But do you?"

She sensed the threat in him and realized he was cold-bloodedly furious. "No." Kelsey dropped her eyes, staring at the first button of his khaki shirt. "No, I don't think you're the blackmailing type."

He straightened, letting his hands fall away from the

wall. Grim-faced, he went back to his chair. "Well, thanks for that much at least."

She glared at his back. "Don't act as if it's such a small matter. Considering your high-handed, strong, silent style, it's a wonder I'm even willing to give you the benefit of a doubt!"

He shot her a mocking glance. "I'll look on it as a small step toward trust."

"A very small step," she flung back, seething.

"Sit down, Kelsey. We've got some talking to do this morning."

"Are you going to tell me what's going on between you and Roger?"

"No." He smiled faintly. "Other than to tell you that it's a personal matter between Roger and me, I'm not going to discuss the subject with you, and you should realize that by now."

She held herself very still for a long moment, reading the implacable set of his face. "Then there's nothing else to talk about, is there?"

"There's last night."

"Really?" She moved determinedly back to the table, reaching for her red checkbook.

"Kelsey, what are you doing?"

"I'm writing out a check for three thousand dollars. That should cover my family's obligation to you for the next three months. During that time I will find out just what in hell is going on, and then I'll decide what to do next."

"Don't be an idiot."

"I've been an idiot for the past month. I'm trying to recover some lost ground." She industriously bent over the check, filling in the blanks and scrawling her name with a flourish.

"Forget the check, damn it, and look at me, Kelsey." He put out a hand to cover her fingers just as she finished signing her name. When she raised her eyes, resentment and wariness clear in them, he went on steadily, "I'm sorry if you were hurt by the fact that I left you alone last night. I honestly didn't know quite how to handle things. I intended to walk over this morning, maybe take you for a long hike on the beach while we discussed the situation. I thought you'd want some time to yourself when you awoke, though. After all, last night you didn't want to talk at all, remember?"

Last night she hadn't wanted to deal with the traumatic emotional events that had just taken place. She had been struggling between a longing to let herself drift in the physically pleasant afterglow of satisfaction and the knowledge that she was involved in a dangerous dilemma. She had chosen to give herself over to the physical languor.

Meeting Cole's steady gaze now, however, Kelsey realized there was no point trying to explain all that to him. There wasn't much use trying to explain anything to a man who didn't believe in open, honest communication.

"I remember," she whispered.

His expression softened and so did his voice. "Last night was good, wasn't it, Kelsey?"

"Depends what you use to judge it," she told him with surprising calm.

He refused to react to the deliberate provocation, shaking his head with a whimsical smile. "I'm judging it by the way you wrapped yourself around me. By the fierce little demands you made. By the way you called my name and by the way you went up in flames in my hands. Going to deny it?"

"No," she said honestly. "By those standards, it was good. Want to know the truth? It was unlike anything else I've ever known. It was fantastic." She got to her feet abruptly, the check in her hand, aware that she had at last managed to take him by surprise. "I'll be sure to call you, Cole, the next time I'm in the mood for a terrifically interesting one-night stand. Here's the three thousand. You can cash the check on Monday. It won't bounce."

"Where do you think you're going?" he snarled as she picked up her checkbook and headed for the door.

"Home."

"What makes you think you can walk out like this?" He was right behind her.

"Common sense." She was almost at the door.

"You know full well you can't end everything between us just by walking out that door!"

"What are you going to do? Tie me up and lock me away here in your fortress?" She reached for the doorknob, aware that her hand was shaking. She wasn't at all certain but that Cole might just do something that crazy. She had to escape from his prison of a home.

"Kelsey, listen to me," he began.

"Anytime you feel like talking, *really* talking, I might just decide to listen. In the meantime I've got better—"

She got no further as his hand clamped down on her shoulder and he spun her around.

"You want a relationship based on total communication? Well, I want one based on total trust."

"You can't have one without the other," she cried.

He seemed to be making an effort to control his temper. "Kelsey, we're both talking in terms of extremes, and that's not the way it has to be. We need to calm down and start over."

"An excellent idea," she agreed very politely.

He searched her face with suspicion. "We need to start over," he repeated cautiously, "but that doesn't mean we can forget what happened last night."

"Don't worry," she told him with great depth of feeling. "I will never forget what happened last night."

"Don't twist my words, Kelsey," he warned. "Last night I made you mine, and there's no going back to a time when you didn't belong to me. That part of the situation remains carved in stone, understand?"

"I hear every arrogant word you're saying."

Something very much like anguish seemed to appear in the normally unreadable gray eyes, startling Kelsey. Whatever the emotion was it disappeared almost at once, and she succeeded in convincing herself it hadn't been there at all. Cole's fingers bit deeply into the persimmon sweater.

"Kelsey, believe me, there are reasons for the rules I've made for myself. It will be better for both of us if you'll just trust me."

"When was the last time you trusted anyone, Cole?" she asked sadly. Before he could respond, she slipped out from under his hand and walked through the door.

Cole stood on the threshold, hands clenched at his sides as he watched her open the heavy iron gate. Her tawny hair danced around her shoulders as she swept out of the garden. He remembered the feminine strength and the softness in her that had been his last night, and he swore under his breath.

She was upset this morning because she'd accidentally come across those financial records of Roger's. Why the devil had the man put them on his computer, Cole wondered in disgust. Perhaps if Kelsey hadn't found that file she would have been in a much different mood this morning.

Or perhaps not, he conceded, slamming the front door of his home and heading back to his unfinished coffee. Kelsey was a cautious little thing, inquisitive and careful.

But last night he had proven to both of them that she was capable of abandoning herself in his arms. It was a start. In bed, at least, he could overcome her wary, prudent approach to their love affair. Given time he could teach her to trust him.

Cole's eyes fell on the check for three thousand dollars, lying on the table. Irritated, he picked it up and tore it into several very small pieces.

Monday he'd call a local travel agency and get himself booked on Kelsey's cruise. A week's vacation at sea might be the perfect way to reestablish the foundation of the affair he intended to have with Kelsey Murdock.

At least on a ship she wouldn't be able to run far.

FOUR

"I want you to know how much I appreciate your dropping these analysis runs off at Valentine's island," Walt Gladwin told Kelsey for what must have been the hundredth time. "You're saving the company a couple of grand in courier's fees. And in addition I'll have the peace of mind of knowing the documents are in good hands."

"It's no problem, Walt. To tell you the truth, I'm somewhat curious about Mr. Valentine and his island. It should be an interesting side trip."

"The guy's a first-class eccentric, but he's also a genuine genius." Walt smiled, stuffing the computer printout sheets into a heavy black-leather attaché case that stood open on his desk. "This set of printouts is evidence of that. It's an analysis of his latest theories. He sent us the theoretical data on artificial intelligence that he wanted put through our computer and we're sending him back the results. They hold tremendous potential. He's making incredible strides in computer technology. He's got his own hardware on the island, but it's only a small, personal computer. He can explore some of his theories on it and work out the logic needed to analyze them, but he needs our mainframe to actually do the analysis of this kind of stuff. You won't have to worry about keeping track of the keys to these locks, by the way. Valentine has his own set. One less thing to think about.''

Privately Kelsey thought the case with its shiny chrome locks looked like something out of a sophisticated fashion magazine for spies. She was going to feel a bit self-conscious carrying the thing aboard ship the next day.

It was typical of Walt Gladwin to supply such an exotic-looking case, however. When it came to personal items, Gladwin always treated himself to the best. One of the outstandingly successful young executives in the volatile world of computer technology, Gladwin had made a great deal of money very quickly, and, as he was fond of telling anyone who was interested, he fully intended to enjoy it while he was in his prime.

Gladwin's clothes were from the trendiest Italian and French designers. His hand-sewn shoes were made of the softest kid leather and his three cars were from three different European nations. Tonight he was driving Kelsey home in her favorite, the Ferrari. The Mercedes was lovely, too, of course, and she couldn't say she didn't like the Lotus. But there was something about the fire-engine-red Ferrari that appealed to her sense of humor.

She needed a bit of humor this evening, Kelsey decided with an inwardly stifled sigh as Walt closed up the office and escorted her out to the parking lot. It had been a long and not particularly fun-filled day in the

office with Walt, readying the last of the documents
she was to take to the man called Valentine.

In addition to the fact that she had put in some long,
hard hours at work, Kelsey was forced to acknowledge
that there had been no call from Cole.

She knew she had been expecting a phone call.

Over and over again she had told herself that the last
thing she wanted was to hear from the man. But another small voice had assured her he wasn't the type
simply to let her walk out the door. He would contact
her. Kelsey had rehearsed several pithy phrases to use
if and when she did hear from him, but to date there
had been no occasion to use any of them.

It was just as well, she reminded herself as Walt
opened the Ferrari door and ushered her inside. Whatever relationship she had hoped to build with Cole
Stockton had been doomed from the beginning.

"Are you all packed?" Walt inquired easily as he piloted the high-strung car out of the parking lot.

"I think so. Just a few last-minute things to go in the
suitcase." She cast a rueful eye on the attaché case.
"Am I supposed to chain that to my wrist?"

Walt grinned, his good-looking features adjusting
readily to the expression. Walt Gladwin was an attractive, open-faced man in his mid-thirties who smiled a
lot. But, then, he had a lot to smile about, Kelsey reflected. Wealthy, successful and handsome, he seemed
to have life in the palm of his hand. He also had a number of women there, too. Kelsey, for reasons she had
never really stopped to analyze, had politely refused
the one or two suggestions Walt had made that she join
those women. Her lack of interest hadn't concerned

Gladwin. He'd cheerfully gone on to the next flower, and Kelsey's relationship with him had remained strictly professional.

"Wouldn't be a bad idea," he mused pleasantly as he turned the Ferrari in the direction of Kelsey's apartment complex.

"You're kidding!" she said, laughing. "Are those reports that valuable?"

"Oh, they're valuable. To the right people, that is. Most folks probably wouldn't have any notion of the real worth, even if they did happen to see them. This artificial intelligence stuff is right out there on the edge of current technology. There are only a handful of people in the world who have any idea of what it's all about."

"They say that when we can teach computers to think like a human and actually make judgments that are based on human-type logic we'll have a whole new generation of machines," Kelsey noted.

"It'll be called the fifth generation. That's what Valentine is working toward." Walt nodded. "But it's a long way off. The small slice of the future we're working on at Flex-Glad is highly theoretical at this point."

"And Valentine is capable of understanding these reports?"

"Valentine created the basic theory on which these analysis sheets and reports are based. He doesn't have access to the kind of computer equipment he needs to test his ideas and theories, so Flex-Glad and Valentine have made a mutually beneficial bargain. We pay him to think and he allows us to test what he dreams up. If and when we hit the jackpot he'll get a share of the profits."

"If he needs access to sophisticated computers in order to verify his work, why does he live on that island?"

"He's a nut," Walt said with a shrug. "A certified eccentric. Who knows how he thinks? If he did his thinking in a normal way he wouldn't be very useful to us."

"I suppose you've got a point. He is expecting me, isn't he?"

"Yes, don't worry. He's made arrangements to meet you at the small landing strip that serves the island."

"Does anyone else live on that island?"

"A few people. Mostly fishermen and their families. From what I understand, Valentine ignores them and they return the favor. It's one of the least developed islands in the Caribbean, and that's saying something. The whole area isn't exactly rich."

"Do I just hand these papers over to him? I mean, should I get him to sign a receipt, or something? How will I know I'm dealing with the right man?" Kelsey asked curiously.

Gladwin chuckled. "There's only one Valentine. I met him a year ago. He's a huge bear of a man with long hair and a beard that falls halfway down his chest. He wears a pair of wire-rimmed glasses and he has an attitude about him that makes you think you're taking up his valuable time. You won't be encouraged to stay. All Valentine wants is to be left alone with his brain and the small computer he's rigged up on that island. Lucky for us he can't install the kind of hardware he needs to test his programs and theories. Otherwise he wouldn't need Flex-Glad. But there's no way he could put the highly sophisticated monsters into his shack. Nor could he afford them."

"He hasn't made a lot of money yet with his theories?"

"Just between you and me, the man's not much of a businessman," Walt confided. "Is this where I turn?"

"Yes, the next street. You can pull into the parking lot and I'll hop out."

Walt looked comically astonished. "What? No bon-voyage drink?"

Kelsey blinked. "Oh. Well, if you'd like to share one with me..."

"Sure. After all, I'm sending you off with a portion of Flex-Glad's future. I think that deserves a drink."

Gladwin parked the Ferrari and jumped out to open Kelsey's door. Together they walked up the stone path to her garden apartment.

"Nice place," Walt said as he glanced around at the small patio while Kelsey dug out her key.

"Thanks. I like it."

"Not as nice as your mother's place in Carmel, though, I'll bet. I'm thinking of picking up some beachfront property down there myself."

He probably would do just that, Kelsey decided as she turned the key in the lock. Walt was indulging himself these days. He might save money wherever he could in business, but he certainly didn't worry about stinting in his personal life.

Carmel was not a place she wanted to think about at the moment, however. The memories of her last night there still haunted her dreams and the pain of that final scene with Cole bit deep.

"Your phone's ringing," Walt observed helpfully as he pushed open the door. "You go ahead and answer it, and I'll see what you've got in your kitchen in the way of farewell toast material."

Kelsey watched him blithely walk into her sunny papaya-and-tan kitchen while she automatically reached for the phone. Walt certainly made himself at home easily. He'd never even been in her apartment before and already he was opening cupboard doors. Cole had a far more restrained attitude about such things, she reflected.

But, then, Cole had been far more restrained and cautious around her in every regard. Until that last night, of course.

Kelsey shivered and spoke quickly into the phone, anxious to erase the small chill that had coursed down her spine.

"Hello?"

There was a pause on the other end and even before she heard the soft, dark voice, Kelsey's instincts sensed the identity of the caller.

"It's about time you got home. It's almost ten o'clock."

"Cole."

Feeling unaccountably shaken, Kelsey sank down onto the leather-and-chrome chair beside the phone. After a week of silence he had decided to call. She wasn't at all certain she wanted to learn why. The palm of her hand grasping the white phone felt damp.

"What do you want, Cole?" Kelsey kept her voice

low, aware of the tension in it. She prayed Walt would busy himself in the kitchen for a few more minutes. Frantically she tried to think how best to handle the situation. All the sharp little phrases she had been practicing seemed to have fled her mind.

"For starters, you could tell me where you've been all evening," he suggested a bit too blandly.

"Working." There, that was definitely short and pithy.

"I see."

"Look, Cole, I can't imagine why you're bothering to call tonight, unless—" She broke off as an overoptimistic thought struck her. "Unless you've finally decided to explain about that file in Roger's computer." She could feel the knot of uncertainty coiling in her stomach.

"You've got a one-track mind, haven't you, honey?" Cole said, sighing. "Well, as it turns out, so do I. Are you alone?"

"No, I'm not," she told him with a fierce hint of defiance. "My boss is having a bon-voyage drink with me. I can't really talk very long, Cole. Please say what you have to say and leave me alone."

"You mean, leave you with Gladwin," Cole growled. "Get rid of him, Kelsey."

Quite deliberately she maintained her silence in the face of the clear-cut command. Damned if she would allow this man to order her around.

"Kelsey? I mean it. You know better than to play this kind of game with me."

"I don't play games, Cole. You're the one who likes games," she accused tightly.

"Nothing," he vowed gently, "that I have ever done to you has been in the nature of a game. And I'm not playing one now. Kelsey, you've been seeing me for a month. Don't you know me well enough yet to realize I won't share you with another man, now that you belong to me?"

Kelsey swallowed, aware of the claim he insisted he had on her. The unpleasant truth was that she did know him well enough to believe he meant every word now. And she had no right to involve Walt in the firefight.

"Did you only call to harass me?" she managed coolly as Walt walked into the living room, holding a bottle of cognac and two glasses. He grinned cheerfully and sat down across from her on the white sofa.

"To be honest," Cole said calmly, "the answer is no. I called to see if you had made arrangements to have your parents' plants taken care of while you're gone. You're leaving tomorrow, aren't you?"

She drew a deep breath. "That's right." With a small smile she accepted the cognac Walt handed to her. "And you don't have to worry about the plants. I notified mom's housekeeper to start looking after them. Thank you for thinking of them, though," she went on in a deliberately chatty tone. "I believe everything's under control. I'll let you know how the trip was when I return. Thanks for calling to wish me goodbye."

Before Cole could respond she gently hung up the phone. "Just a neighbor calling to say so long," she explained lightly to Walt.

"Well, here's to a fun trip for you and a potentially profitable one for Flex-Glad," Walt said pleasantly, lifting his glass in a toast. "Be sure to send us all a postcard."

"Of Valentine?" she teased.

He laughed. "Never mind Valentine. Pick a shot of a nude beach. Much more interesting."

She was going to have to get rid of him quickly, Kelsey thought. Poor Walt. He had no idea of how he'd just been caught in the cross fire. But he was a nice man and she couldn't bring herself to involve him further.

True, Cole had been calling from Carmel and there wasn't much he could do about Walt tonight, but she instinctively knew that wasn't much protection for her boss in the future. She'd already had a sample of Cole's potential for violence and she knew just how implacable he could be. He had told her to get rid of Walt and—uneasily—Kelsey decided to do exactly that. It would be much safer for everyone, including herself.

God, she was letting Cole's threats get to her. A week of wondering if he would pursue the relationship as he had promised must have eaten away a portion of her brain.

But she had unfinished business with Cole Stockton, and until it was cleared up she had an obligation to keep others out of harm's way.

Fifteen minutes later Kelsey had politely maneuvered her boss to the door.

"Don't let that attaché case out of your sight, Kelsey," Walt warned on an unexpectedly serious note just as she was about to close the door.

"Don't worry, I'll take good care of it," she promised.

"I don't doubt that for a minute," he said with a grin,

lifting a hand in farewell. "You're just about the best administrative assistant I've ever had. Take care and have a good trip."

The phone rang again just as Kelsey firmly shut and locked the door. With a sense of deep foreboding she picked up the receiver.

"Is he gone?" Cole asked blandly.

"What do you think?"

"I think he is."

He sounded so disgustingly sure of himself that Kelsey wanted to scream. It took a strong effort of will to hang on to her temper. "Then why bother calling back?" she asked politely.

"Just for the reassurance, I suppose."

"I didn't think you were the kind of man who needed any reassurances," she snapped. "You always seem so very damn sure of yourself."

There was a slight hesitation before Cole asked quietly, "Would you believe me if I told you there are times when you make me feel a little uncertain?"

"No," she retorted flatly. "Any man who has learned to put up the kind of walls you've built for yourself and your house hasn't got room for any emotion as soft and wishy-washy as uncertainty. Good night, again, Cole."

Very firmly Kelsey replaced the receiver, and then she unplugged the phone. Her mouth curving ruefully at the small, probably meaningless act of defiance, she headed for the bedroom to finish her packing.

The following evening Cole flicked another glance at the face of the stainless-steel watch on his wrist. It was nearly nine o'clock and Kelsey still had not made an appearance. She had not shown up for the second seating at dinner, which was just ending, and there had been no sign of her earlier in any of the three cocktail lounges. Cole had checked them all.

He had wound up sharing dinner with the other couple who had been assigned to his table. June and George Camden were pleasant enough, even though one could get tired of hearing of George's exploits on the golf course. But the cheerful middle-aged couple certainly hadn't made up for the empty place across from Cole.

He had tipped well to have Kelsey reassigned to his table, but she, apparently, had had something better to do this evening than join the rest of the passengers in the main dining salon.

If he had been a less controlled man, Cole's fingers would have been drumming restlessly on the white tablecloth. Or perhaps he would have begun to snap his responses to George Camden's running monologue on golf courses he had known and loved.

But Cole allowed none of his growing unease and impatience to show. He knew she was on the ship. He had watched her come aboard late that afternoon in Puerto Rico. She had arrived in San Juan to catch the liner about an hour after he had. He hadn't seen her since she had disappeared with a cabin steward in the direction of her stateroom. Quite deliberately Cole had kept out of sight, wanting to time his appearance.

"Will you be going on to one of the lounges after dinner, Cole?" June Camden asked politely. "The entertainment should be starting soon."

"There's always a nice variety of young women looking for a little fun and games on these ships," George advised with a wink. "If I were you I'd take advantage of the opportunities available. The trick is to get moving before the ship's officers have picked out the best of the bunch."

"George!" his wife exclaimed in vast annoyance. "What a horrid way to talk! As if you knew!"

"Remember, I'm a golfer, my dear," George pointed out complacently. "I'm quite capable of observing the way the ball lies."

June got determinedly to her feet. Her comfortably rounded figure was sheathed in a vividly patterned silk dress of green and turquoise that set off the equally vivid blue of her lively eyes. "I think you will have to excuse us, Cole. It's time I took George into the nearest bar and bought him a drink. A few Scotch and sodas and he'll decide I still look good enough to dance with."

Cole gave her a serious, intent smile. "Believe me, June, you look good enough for that right now and I haven't even had any Scotch and sodas."

June laughed, delighted, and George arched bushy gray brows in mock warning as he rose beside his wife. "Hands off, my boy. You'll have to find a woman of your own tonight. This one's already spoken for!"

"Oh, George," and June chuckled, clearly pleased.

"Have a good evening," Cole said politely as they took their leave. "Perhaps I'll see you around later. After I've found my own lady for the evening."

"Good luck," George said, grinning.

Luck, Cole reflected as he watched them leave,

should have nothing to do with it. Everything had been carefully engineered from his end. If there was one factor he did not like to have to depend on, it was luck. But something had gone wrong tonight. Kelsey should have been sitting opposite him all during dinner. What the hell had gone wrong?

Perhaps George was right. Maybe one of the ship's officers or a fellow passenger had already made his move. Cole rose, his face set in a cold, hard expression that made the hovering steward fear for his tip at the end of the cruise.

If she hadn't been hungry she might have spent the past couple of hours browsing around the huge luxury vessel, Cole told himself. He'd start with the sun deck and work down, systematically checking all the public rooms and lounges. She had to be somewhere on board.

With a methodical approach he moved from one deck to the next, pushing through a crowd of disco dancers in one lounge and then forging a path through the small gambling casino that had just opened up for the evening. From there he wandered outside to search the floodlit pool area.

It took quite a while to convince himself he'd covered every possible public place on board, but in the end Cole had to admit Kelsey wasn't anywhere to be found.

Surely she wouldn't have spent the first evening in her small stateroom, he told himself, realizing there was nowhere else to look. A woman like Kelsey didn't book herself onto an expensive Caribbean cruise and then sit alone in her room the first night out!

Still, he had pursued every other possible option. He might as well check her stateroom. Cole took the ship's elevator to the fourth deck and paced along the carpeted hall. He'd calmly bribed a cabin steward to get her room number earlier. It hadn't been a problem. Cole knew how to get information when he needed it.

Cabin number 4063 was one in a long row of outside staterooms. Cole paused in front of the orange door and found himself hesitating a fraction of a second before he knocked.

The faint twinge of uncertainty that stayed his hand was irritating but not unexpected. He was learning just what thoughts of Kelsey Murdock could do to him. The biggest question now was how she would react when she realized he was on board. He knocked on the cabin door.

There was a faint shuffling movement inside, and then a very low voice begged softly, "Please go away. I told you I didn't want any dinner."

Frowning at the weak sound of Kelsey's mumbled words, Cole knocked again. "Kelsey? Are you all right?"

There was another sound of movement and then the door was opened a distance of about three inches. One very weary, hazel-green eye stared at him balefully.

"Oh, my God," Kelsey breathed in shock. "Now I'm hallucinating." She slammed the door.

Prepared for that eventuality, Cole had thrust his foot over the threshold. "Kelsey, what's wrong? I was wondering what had happened to you."

Inside the small room, Kelsey leaned back against the door, fully aware she was too weak to counter the steady pressure he was applying. This was all she needed, she thought morosely. On top of everything else, Cole Stockton was on board ship with her.

"Kelsey, let me in."

The force of his one-handed push sent the door swinging inward. Kelsey was propelled forward. She managed to maintain herself in an upright position by grasping frantically for the edge of the bathroom door. It stood conveniently open because she had already made several trips through it.

Turning to glare at him, Kelsey found herself oddly distracted by the dark, powerful image he made dressed in a formal black evening jacket and a gray dress shirt. His deep-brown hair was combed into the familiar severe style.

By contrast she felt distinctly rumpled and frumpy. Her hair was hanging in tangled tendrils and her peach-colored bathrobe was knotted untidily. She knew she looked drawn and pale. Valiantly she struggled for her self-possession.

"This is a tropical cruise," she noted dryly. "Couldn't you have found something else besides a black dinner jacket? Something a little lighter in color? White socks might have added a nice touch."

"You know me and my limited wardrobe," he remarked, eyeing her closely. "But right now I'll have to say that I'm better dressed for life on a cruise ship than you are. What's the matter, Kelsey?"

She was too drained to make even a token protest of his presence. "I've never been at sea before." She closed her eyes briefly. "Apparently I'm not much of a sailor. Excuse me, Cole. I have a date with the bathroom." She lurched through the open door as another wave of nausea assailed her.

Cole was beside her instantly. "Take it easy, honey. It'll be all right," he soothed gently, holding her as the spasms shook her body.

"Go away," she pleaded. "Let me die in peace."

"You're not going to die."

"You don't know that for sure. Oh, Lord, I feel awful."

"As soon as I get you back to bed I'll dig up the ship's doctor. He'll be able to give you something for the seasickness. Here, let me wash your face."

She stood like a sick child, meekly allowing him to rinse her face and hands. Then he prepared her toothbrush with a dab of minty toothpaste and wrapped her fingers around the handle. "You'll feel better if you brush your teeth," he advised.

"How do you know?" she muttered belligerently. But she obeyed the soft command in his voice and leaned over the wash basin. "If only this ship would stop moving. Why didn't someone tell me it would be like this?"

"Because most people don't have any problems on a perfectly calm sea," Cole murmured, handing her a glass of water. "After you rinse your mouth out I want you to drink a little of this."

"I couldn't possibly," she groaned, staring at the glass as though it were a snake.

"Just a few sips. How long have you been sick?"

"Since an hour after I came on board."

"Then you're bound to be somewhat dehydrated. Take a couple of sips of water, Kelsey."

"It'll just come right back up," she warned miserably.

"Give it a chance," he urged, holding the glass to her pale lips.

She saw the concern in his smoky eyes as she obediently took two small swallows of water, and the knowledge that he was actually worried about her health fascinated her for a moment. "What are you doing here, Cole? You're supposed to be safe behind your high stone walls back in Carmel."

"Around you I find myself willing to take a few risks," he growled. "That's enough water. Now back to bed while I go dig the doctor out of the cocktail lounge."

"How do you know that's where he'll be?" She allowed herself to be guided across the small room to the single bed. She wasn't particularly surprised that Cole's arms felt strong and supportive, but she was vaguely astounded they also felt rather reassuring.

"Where would you hang out on the first night of a cruise if you were the ship's doctor? The infirmary?"

"Well, no, I guess not. Oh, Cole, I have never felt so terrible in my whole life. I just want to get off this ship and go home. Maybe I'll throw myself overboard."

"You'll feel entirely different in the morning. Trust me."

"I can't. I hardly know you, remember?" Kelsey wasn't quite sure where she found the energy for the small spurt of resentment. Given the way she felt, she was startled she could summon up even such a minor act of rebellion.

"The lady has a one-track mind," Cole said with a

sigh as he tucked her into bed. "Stay put until I find the doctor, okay?"

"Believe me, I'm not going anywhere in my present condition."

A small smile crooked Cole's mouth as he stood looking down at her. "If you were always this cooperative, I wouldn't have any problems."

"I am not amused," Kelsey tried to say regally.

"I'll be right back." Cole turned to leave, and the toe of his shoe struck the black-leather attaché case sitting beside the bed. "Ah, let me guess. I'll bet that's Gladwin's little courier pack, isn't it? The one you're supposed to take to the kooky genius?"

"I've been instructed not to let it out of my sight. Lord, Cole, if I don't feel better by the day after tomorrow I may not be alive to deliver the papers!"

"I keep telling you to trust me," he muttered as he walked out the door.

Kelsey lay with her eyes closed, dreading each gentle movement of the ship, and wondered bleakly at what point during his mysterious past Cole had learned to be such a good nurse.

He certainly wasn't the squeamish type. But she couldn't help wondering if any man could maintain much interest in a woman who looked like death warmed over. A man in love might be able to handle his lover in the throes of seasickness, she decided grimly, but what about a man who was only interested in hiring a mistress? Her stomach turned violently at that moment, successfully changing the focus of her thoughts.

Cole arrived with the doctor who was young, good-looking and possessed of a brilliant bedside manner.

"Believe me, you're going to feel like a new woman in the morning," he promised cheerfully as he filled a hypodermic needle. "This stuff will fix you right up. Wouldn't want you to spend the cruise here in your bunk. Over you go now."

"Over where? Over the side?" Kelsey gritted her teeth as another wave of sickness threatened to consume her.

"Over on your stomach," the doctor said, chuckling, standing with the needle at the ready.

"Uh, couldn't you give me the shot in my arm?" she asked uncertainly, conscious of Cole's standing a foot away.

"Come on, honey, let's get it over with." Cole glided forward, sitting down beside her and pulling her lightly into his lap. Gently he smoothed aside the robe.

Kelsey swore softly and turned her face into his black jacket as the doctor delivered the medication. She felt abused and annoyed and embarrassed. In her disgruntled state of mind it was easy to suddenly blame Cole for the entire situation. If there had been even a hint of sensuality in his touch on her bare thigh, Kelsey would have bitten him. There was nothing but firm gentleness, however.

"That should take care of everything, Ms. Murdock. I'm sure I'm leaving you in capable hands. Check in with me in the morning if you have any further problems. I can give you some tablets if you need them. I have a hunch you'll be fine, however. Good night."

"It's okay for him to be so damn cheerful. He's

headed back to the bar, I'll bet," Kelsey groaned. Hastily she readjusted her robe and wriggled off Cole's lap. "And I'm sure that's where you'd like to go, too. Thank you for the help, Cole. Please don't worry about me. I'll be all right. You've done more than enough."

But Cole was already getting to his feet and shrugging out of his jacket. "I'll stay until you're safely asleep. The doctor said the stuff he gave you would put you out like a light."

"Really, Cole, there's no need—"

"Honey, you're in no shape to kick me out, so you might as well accept the inevitable gracefully." He hung the jacket in her closet and came back to the bed.

Kelsey lay staring up at him through slitted lashes, absorbing the impact of his solid, dark presence here in her tiny shipboard bedroom. Through the welter of sensations, both physical and mental, that she had been experiencing during the past few hours, she suddenly realized that everything about her association with Cole Stockton took on overtones of inevitability.

Looking back, it seemed inevitable that they should meet. Having met, it seemed equally inevitable that he should have seduced her. And after the seduction it seemed inevitable that he should claim her as his own. Therefore, her blurry mind decided, it was probably inevitable that he should be standing here in her room.

"I think that shot the doctor gave me is affecting my brain," she told Cole drowsily.

"Were you really surprised to see me, honey?" Cole asked softly, as though he'd read her mind. "You shouldn't have been. You should have known I'd come after you."

"You didn't show much interest during the past week," she tried to say flippantly. "You called only once."

"And found you having a farewell drink with Gladwin."

She heard the hardening in his voice and took refuge in her illness. "Oh, Cole, my stomach..."

Immediately he hunkered down beside the bunk. "Want me to carry you into the bathroom?"

"No, I, uh, think I'll be all right this time. I'm feeling very sleepy, though." She closed her eyes, relieved to have found a way around the faint menace that had crept into his words. It was far more pleasant to have Cole in this helpful, concerned mood. "You're rather good at this nursing business. You must have done it sometime during your past, hmm?" Even on the verge of sleep, her body feeling devastated by the seasickness, Kelsey still found herself struggling for information about this man. She was drawn to him like a moth to a flame.

"No, Kelsey, I was never a nurse."

She thought there was a tinge of amusement in his tone, but she could no longer be sure. She could no longer be certain of anything, in fact. The blurriness in her mind seemed to be overwhelming her thought processes. Sleep beckoned as an escape after hours of fighting the seasickness, and she gave into it with a vast sense of relief.

She awoke only once during the night, turning sleepily onto her side in the dimly lit room. Cole had switched off all the lights except the small one over the dresser. He was still here, she thought, aware of a deep sense of comfort at the knowledge.

He stood in front of the dresser, reading intently. Perhaps he'd found a magazine. She started to close her eyes again and was almost asleep, when something registered on her drowsy brain.

The black leather attaché case stood open on the floor beside him. The papers he was examining must have come from the case.

The attaché case had been locked, she thought, unable to fight the pull of the drug-induced sleep. She knew it had been locked. Big, shiny chrome locks that Walt Gladwin had closed. He hadn't given her the keys, saying that Valentine had a set of his own.

Cole had no right to be prying into that case, Kelsey tried to tell herself, but it was useless to struggle against the pleasant oblivion that was claiming her. She sank heavily back into the depths of slumber.

FIVE

Kelsey was immediately aware of two things the moment she awoke: the first was that Cole wasn't in the
room and the second was that her stomach felt calm. It
was some time before she realized the black attaché
case was gone. She was on her way to the shower, glorying in her victory over the seasickness, when she remembered the midnight vision of Cole poring over the
contents of the attaché case.

Half-convinced the memory was a dream, she automatically glanced around for the case. It wasn't in the
room.

Brow furrowing in concentration, she checked the
small closet, glanced under the bunk and then yanked
open the dresser drawers. Nothing. Surely Cole
wouldn't have taken it. He could have no possible interest in a bunch of computer printouts and analysis
sheets. And she must have imagined that late-night
scene of Cole studying the papers.

This morning what she really wanted to remember
was the way he had taken care of her last night. She
had awakened with a sense of loss at the realization

that he wasn't with her. During the night he had offered comfort and practical assistance. His touch had been gentle and soothing.

She certainly hadn't looked like anyone's idea of a glamorous mistress last night, Kelsey reminded herself as she gave up the search for the case and went on into the bathroom. There was no denying that Cole's concern had been deeply comforting. Somehow it had soothed much of the inner anger and resentment she had been experiencing all week.

She ought to have known better. After all, Kelsey thought savagely, nothing had changed in their relationship. She knew no more about him than she ever had.

Except now she knew he could deal very competently with a sick female.

And what had he done with her attaché case, she wondered nervously. For that matter, where was Cole? One thing was certain, she thought with dark humor: he couldn't have got off the ship. They had been underway all night and weren't due to dock in a port until tomorrow morning.

Again she thought of his actions during the previous evening. She had been too ill to be terribly astonished at the sight of him. Instead she had decided that his presence was inevitable. At least that was the way it had seemed to her weary brain last night.

Now she had to ask herself just why Cole had followed her and why he had taken care of her. And most of all why he had broken into the attaché case.

The conclusions she was forced to arrive at in the shower were nerve-racking. Walt had said the information in that case was extremely valuable but that only a handful of people could understand it. He certainly hadn't implied that anyone might resort to stealing it.

Cole had never seemed particularly interested in computers in general, but they had spent a lot of time talking about her job, Kelsey reminded herself anxiously.

But she had met him so casually! There had been nothing suspiciously coincidental about it. Or so she assumed. He had simply been a reclusive man who had eventually made friends with his next-door neighbors and, ultimately, with their daughter.

He hadn't even known she worked for Flex-Glad until after he had met her. Unless her stepfather had mentioned it, she added in silent anguish.

God, she was going crazy this morning, trying to figure out the whole mess. She had to get control of herself and the situation. The first order of business was to get back that attaché case. Walt had entrusted her with it. She couldn't bear to confess she had been stupid enough to get seduced by an industrial spy who had now stolen the data she was supposed to deliver to Valentine.

Nor could she bear to believe that Cole would do such a thing to her. Kelsey shuddered as she slipped into a white collarless linen shirt and matching wide-legged linen pants. Sliding her feet into a pair of bright-red sandals, she paused to run a brush through her hair and clip the tawny stuff back behind her ears.

She had to keep things in perspective. With those words of caution echoing in her head, Kelsey left her stateroom and headed for the dining room. For the first time since she had arrived on board she found herself thinking about food.

Perhaps after a cup of coffee she would be able to sort out the truth of the situation. Then she would confront Cole and demand some explanations. This time he wasn't going to get away with simply refusing to discuss certain subjects, she promised herself.

The sea air was fresh and invigorating. This morning the endless blue waters were a delight to the eye. Sunlight danced on the waves and the gentle motion of the ship no longer bothered her. The day was already turning warm. Kelsey took a brisk walk on deck before seeking out the dining room. It was still early, and only a handful of people were at breakfast. She saw Cole almost immediately.

Kelsey hesitated at the realization that she was going to have to deal with him before she'd had the promised coffee and more time to think. Then her natural spirit surged to the surface. Lifting her chin, she walked straight toward the table where he sat alone. Cole watched her come toward him, a politely unreadable expression on his hard face.

"Good morning, Kelsey. We have the table to ourselves. The Camdens appear to be late risers. How are you feeling?" He got to his feet to hold her chair.

"Much better, thank you," she declared with a breeziness she was far from feeling as she accepted the chair. "Where's the attaché case?"

He blinked lazily under her steady, demanding gaze. But he made no move to sidetrack her. "It's safe enough for the moment."

Kelsey took a deep breath. "I want it back, Cole. And I also want back all the papers that were inside."

He handed her the breakfast menu and said casually, "You act as though you think I might have stolen something, Kelsey. Be careful what you say next."

"Have you stolen anything, Cole?" she asked stonily. "I saw you looking at the printouts that were in that case."

His gray eyes chilled. "Do you believe I'd take them from you?"

"I'm asking because, as usual with you, I don't know what to believe!"

Cole reached for the silver coffeepot that had been set on the table. "Are you ever going to trust me, Kelsey?"

"I told you once you couldn't have trust without genuine communication," she bit out tightly. Kelsey leaned forward. "I want that case back. I have a responsibility to deliver it. I do not want to have to admit to myself or to Walt Gladwin that I allowed a man who had seduced me to make off with those printouts. If you have any respect or...affection for me at all, Cole, you will stop playing games and give me back that case."

He stared at her intently for a long moment, studying her tense features. "And if you trusted me at all you wouldn't accuse me of industrial espionage."

Kelsey paled, but her voice stayed even. "I guess we know where we stand with each other, then, don't we? All the evidence would seem to indicate you've taken advantage of me."

"Do you truly believe that? Last week you accused

me of blackmailing your stepfather. Now I'm supposedly a thief. Last night you didn't think so badly of me. But if you are prepared to make accusations this morning why don't you call a ship's officer and do it right?"

Kelsey bit her lip and shifted restlessly in the chair. "I don't think there's any need to go that far. Just give me back the case and we'll forget about the whole thing."

"No, we will not forget about the whole thing. If you honestly believe I've stolen those printouts, then do something about it. Call an officer and report it. A search will be made of my room and the case will be found. You will identify it and that will be that. You'll probably be able to press charges when we get home." Cole smiled one of his rare smiles, but his eyes were colder than ever. "Go ahead, Kelsey. Act on your beliefs. Make a formal accusation."

"Stop it," she told him, infuriated at the way he was pushing her. She couldn't report him, and he must have known that. "I don't want any dramatic scenes. I just want that case. If it's in your room we can go and get it after breakfast. I won't ask you why you took it—"

"How forebearing of you," he mocked.

"Damn it, how would you feel this morning if the situation were reversed? If you'd seen me going through the contents of that case in the middle of the night and then awakened to find it gone?"

"This reminds me of the conversation we had last week," he mused as a chilled grapefruit was set in front of him. "At that time you were asking me how I'd react if I discovered someone was blackmailing one of my relatives."

"I'm trying to make you understand how ridiculous it is of you to keep demanding that I take everything you say or won't say on trust!"

"Are you going to order breakfast?" he interrupted gently as the steward hovered.

"The last thing I'm thinking about at the moment is breakfast!" she raged stiffly.

Cole glanced up at the waiter. "You can bring her some poached eggs and toast. She was a little seasick last night, so I think we'll keep it simple."

"Yes, sir," the man responded respectfully.

"Cole," Kelsey began as the steward disappeared. "Please stop harassing me. I don't understand you. What do you want from me?"

"You know what I want from you." He calmly started eating the pink grapefruit.

"The printouts?" she challenged.

With great care he put down his spoon. "No, Kelsey, I do not want the printouts. I want you."

"Really?" she retorted sardonically. "Then why take the printouts instead?"

He looked at her with steel in his eyes. "I've told you that if you think I've stolen those printouts, you'd better do something about it. Are you going to call a ship's officer and report me, or not?"

"Don't you dare push me, Cole," she blazed.

"I am pushing you, lady. Either make a formal accusation or stop threatening me. You're ruining my breakfast."

"What do you think you're doing to mine?" she wailed furiously.

"I'm the guy who made it possible for you to eat again this morning, remember? If it hadn't been for me you'd still be lying in your bunk in between running to the bathroom!"

"Cole, you're being utterly ridiculous, expecting me to accept your actions without any explanation."

"There's an explanation. There's always an explanation. Blame yourself for not being able to see it."

"I'm blaming you!" she snapped, outraged.

"So it would seem. So do something or shut up. Call a ship's officer or else let me eat my breakfast in peace."

"You're so damned unreasonable."

"Is it unreasonable to want a little trust from the woman I've asked to come and live with me?"

"This is hardly a 'little' trust, and you're out of your mind if you think your offer is anything terrific in the first place."

"You're getting a bit loud, Kelsey," he pointed out.

"So why don't you do something about it? Call a ship's officer and complain," she suggested, throwing his challenge back in his face.

"You know, I think you were more pleasant when you were sick to your stomach." Cole set down his grapefruit spoon with deliberation. He folded his arms on the white tablecloth and assumed his familiar, aloofly alert expression. "Well? What are you going to do?"

Kelsey had never experienced such a combination of fury and exasperation in her entire life. She ought to take him up on his dare, go ahead and report him to someone in authority. After all, she'd seen him examining the contents of that case and he'd admitted he'd taken it. Why she was hesitating was beyond her.

But she knew, even as she sat there infuriated, that she wasn't going to report him as a thief. What really unnerved her was that Cole probably knew it, too.

"Kelsey?" he prodded softly.

"Eat your breakfast in peace, Cole. You know damn well I'm not going to turn you in for stealing that case." The emotion drained out of her, Kelsey threw down her napkin and made to rise. Cole's hand swept out in a smooth movement, closing around one of her wrists with a pressure that kept her anchored in her seat. His strength could be quite appalling, she thought distantly, staring at his fingers.

"Why aren't you going to call for help, Kelsey?" he asked huskily

"Probably because I'm a fool." She refused to meet his eyes, continuing to stare down at her trapped wrist.

"You're not a fool and we both know it. So why aren't you yelling for the captain?"

That brought her head up proudly. "Why don't you tell me?"

"All right, I will," he said, surprising her by agreeing. "I think you're going to back off from doing anything rash this time for the same reason you didn't scream blackmail to the authorities last week. The same reason you got rid of Gladwin so quickly the other evening after I called. You belong to me now, Kelsey, and on some level I think you recognize that. Our battles are too private, too intimate to allow you to drag others into them. Furthermore, I think you trust me more than you even realize."

"I don't know what could possibly give you that impression," she gasped, ignoring the rest of his words.

"Last night gave me that impression." His expression softened slightly. "You let me take care of you last night, honey. I saw the way you looked at me just before you went to sleep. You weren't frightened of me, were you?"

"I was too sick to waste any energy being frightened," she argued. But it was true. She had found his presence vastly comforting. Even when she'd awakened in the middle of the night and discovered him going through the attaché case she hadn't had the sense to be worried. It wasn't until morning had arrived and she'd realized both he and the case were gone that she'd started questioning his actions.

"Kelsey, deep down do you really believe I've stolen your precious attaché case?"

"Cole, this is not a good time to push me," she gritted, not wanting to be forced into answering.

"I can't seem to find a good time so it will have to be now. Tell me the truth, honey."

She sucked in her breath, knowing she was thoroughly trapped. "I expect you've got some justification for what you did," she temporized coldly.

His mouth crooked wryly. "Your generosity overwhelms me."

"Will you at least give me this much, Cole?" she asked tightly. "Just tell me why you took the case."

Impatience flickered in his eyes, and his voice hardened. "Because I don't like the idea of Gladwin forcing you to chaperon a locked case, that's why. For God's sake, Kelsey, anything that has to be kept under double locks must be valuable. This whole situation bothers me. It has since you first mentioned it. I decided to take the case to my room so that you would no longer have to be responsible for it. Couldn't you have figured that much out for yourself?"

"I saw you looking at the papers inside that case," she whispered.

"Simple curiosity. I wanted to know whether you were carrying anything that could get you into trouble. That's the only reason I opened the case. If it's any consolation, I'm no wiser than I was before I opened it. Those printouts look like so much gibberish."

She considered that broodingly, knowing that, for some totally irrational reason, she actually believed him. The man was so calmly arrogant about the whole situation, though. It made her want to keep pushing and prying and demanding, even when common sense told her she'd probably gone far enough. You'd have thought that by now she would have learned to observe the strict limits Cole set, Kelsey reminded herself.

"Simple curiosity got you through two very sophisticated locks without using keys?" Kelsey remarked with mocking politeness.

"Curiosity is a powerful motivator," he murmured equally politely.

"You are an unreasonable, incomprehensible, totally frustrating man," she said with a sigh, knowing she was beaten.

"Who wants you very much," he added.

Kelsey flushed under the coolly sensual remark.

"But not badly enough to risk a little honest, open communication."

Cole shook his head wryly as her plate of poached eggs and toast was set down along with his mushroom omelet. "Kelsey, honey, you are the victim of all that junk pop psychology that's always being pushed in the media. I can't imagine where everyone got the notion that total communication was always a great thing."

"You're saying you don't believe in honesty?" she gritted, relieved the eggs were actually tasting good and that her stomach was accepting them without a whimper.

"I'm saying I believe more strongly in the right to privacy," he returned easily.

"You certainly weren't respecting my boss's right to privacy when you went through those printouts last night!"

"That's different."

"How?" she demanded forcefully.

"It involves you. Your rights are far more important to me than those of Walt Gladwin. I don't want you being used."

"I am not being used. I am carrying out a small task for my employer. And you had no right to get into that case without permission! Furthermore," she declared recklessly, "if anyone's guilty of using me in the recent past, it's you, not Walt!"

A warning flashed in Cole's eyes, but his voice was silky smooth. "You'd rather be used by an employer than by a lover?"

"At least I get paid by my employer!" Kelsey shot back without pausing to think. She regretted the rash words the moment they were out, but it was far too late.

"I told you last week, I'm willing to pay," he reminded her with a devastating coldness.

Kelsey felt the blood drain from her face. Her stomach, which had been accepting the toast and eggs without complaint, tightened into a savage knot. "Yes, you did, didn't you," she murmured, carefully folding her napkin and setting it beside her plate. "How could I possibly forget your generous offer of bed and board? Excuse me, Cole, I seem to have lost my appetite."

Cole said nothing as she got to her feet and walked out of the dining room. But silently he called himself every name he could think of that meant blundering idiot.

On the other hand, he asked himself savagely, what choice did he have? He wasn't going to unlock all the doors he had closed, not even for Kelsey Murdock. She wouldn't like what she found behind them, anyway. Damn it to hell, why couldn't the woman leave well enough alone? Why did she have to keep pushing and provoking until he found himself deliberately retaliating the way he had a moment ago?

Reminding her of his offer to compensate her for the salary she would lose when she came to live with him was not exactly his brightest move lately. He had already learned she didn't think much of his proposal.

Cole's eyes narrowed as he gazed unseeingly out the nearby dining-salon window. The situation was complicated, but he had the rest of the week to reestablish the basis of the affair.

It was far from hopeless, he told himself. He'd had

some proof lately that when it came down to the bottom line, Kelsey knew whose woman she really was. The way she had responded to him the night he had made love to her, the way she had obeyed him the other evening when he'd phoned and discovered Gladwin was with her and the way she had trusted him to take care of her last night. All the reasons he had listed for her earlier were valid.

But she was hung up on this communication business. Cole went back to his omelet while he considered that roadblock. He'd either have to find a way around it or he'd demolish it.

Because one thing was certain: no one was allowed past the gates that guarded his past. He was a different man now, a man Kelsey could respect and to whom she could give herself without reservation once she accepted the situation. The past had been put behind him by an act of will. He intended to keep it there.

He could allow her some time, but he could not allow her any real choice in the end. Cole didn't kid himself. He wanted her, but more than that he needed her. She was the element that would complete his new life, an element he'd sensed vaguely had been missing but that he hadn't been able to define until he'd met her.

He'd be a fool to let her escape, Cole knew. A lot of people had called him a great many names in the past, but no one had ever labeled him a fool. Foolishness and survival did not go together. Cole was a survivor.

Kelsey found a lounger on the sun deck and flung herself into it. She had brought a magazine to peruse, but it was proving impossible to concentrate. From beneath the canvas awning that provided shade for this portion of the deck she idly watched the bright bikinis and swimsuits gather at poolside. White-jacketed stewards circulated platters of iced tea and rum punches to the cheerful crowd as bodies coated with tanning oil glistened in the sun.

Still feeling a little weak from her ordeal the day before, Kelsey had opted not to go swimming this morning. Today the gentle swells of the sea were beautiful to behold, instead of nausea inducing, she thought with wry amusement. Tomorrow they would be docking in St. Thomas, one of the U.S. Virgin Islands. From there she would take her short charter hop to Valentine's little island.

Always assuming she could get that damned attaché case back from Cole, she added disgustedly. She ought to have put up more of a battle to repossess that case. Instead she had allowed him to send her fleeing from the dining room.

Well, perhaps she hadn't exactly fled, she consoled herself. She had simply walked away from the insult he had delivered. The problem was, Cole didn't seem to understand that what he was offering was an insult.

Perhaps he'd never asked a woman to give up everything and come and live with him. She had no way of knowing what his previous history was with women because she had no way of knowing anything about his previous history, period.

As usual, total frustration set in on that thought, and Kelsey deliberately opened her magazine. She tried very hard to read the fashion article in front of her, but all she could think of was the conflict she was experiencing internally.

Kelsey knew she had been hoping that the cruise would provide the time she needed to make the break psychologically with Cole. She had been counting on the change of atmosphere and the change of pace to enable her to put her life back in perspective.

Now he was here, making all that impossible. She might as well face the fact that this week was going to be one of the most difficult of her life. She had to deal with it because there was no longer any way to run from it. He had seen to that.

"I brought you some iced tea." Cole materialized behind her and took the empty lounger on her left. He set the glass of tea down within her reach. "Not going swimming?"

"How do you manage to sneak up on people so quietly, Cole?" she demanded, asking the first question that popped into her head as she met his eyes. As usual, she hadn't even heard his approach.

He studied her with a flicker of wariness, obviously surprised by her words. "Soft-soled shoes?" he offered hopefully.

His flippancy infuriated her. "Can't you even answer a simple question like that one?"

"Hey," he pleaded, holding up a hand in a placating gesture, "I'm sorry. I didn't mean to be evasive."

"You're always evasive."

"That's not true," he pointed out reproachfully. "I never evade your questions. Sometimes I simply refuse to answer them. There's a difference. In any event, this time around I asked you a question first."

"To which the answer is self-evident," she muttered. "No, I am not going swimming this morning. And it looks like you're not, either," she added, glancing at the rolled-up sleeves of his khaki shirt. "Wearing your normal daytime attire, I see. Delightfully neutral khaki. Don't you have a pair of khaki swim trunks?" she asked innocently.

"If you hadn't been so ill last night, I'd be tempted to put you across my knee. Drink some of your iced tea, honey, and stop trying to bait me. It could be hazardous to your health."

"The tea or baiting you?"

"Guess," he suggested dryly.

"Threats, Cole?" she dared, driven by some indefinable desire to provoke him. It was always like this around him. She felt she had to keep pushing until she found out what made him tick. Incredibly stupid, of course. No woman in her right mind went around probing time bombs to find out what made them tick.

"If they are, I think you know me well enough to be sure they aren't idle ones."

Kelsey glared at him and made a show of returning to her magazine article as if he didn't exist.

"You see, Kelsey?" Cole went on almost cheerfully, "You know more about me than you think. You know when to quit."

It was the amusement in his voice that got to her. "On top of everything else, Cole, please don't laugh at me."

She felt him tighten beside her on the lounger. Aware of the sudden tension in him, Kelsey felt a pang of remorse. Cole's attempts at humor were rare enough as it was. For some crazy reason she wished she hadn't squelched this last poor attempt.

"I am not laughing at you, Kelsey," he told her quietly.

"Then what were you doing?" She set down the magazine and met his eyes very squarely.

"Trying to lighten the situation, I suppose." He leaned back in the lounger with a rather wry curve to his mouth.

"Why bother?"

"I wanted this cruise to be a fresh start for us, honey." He was watching the swimmers, not her face.

Kelsey experienced another wave of inner regret. For one solid month she had wanted nothing more than to have her relationship with Cole succeed. After the traumatic events of last weekend she had told herself nothing could salvage the situation between them. Yet here she was, longing to believe there might be hope. The knowledge that Cole still wanted her seemed to cut through all the rational reasons why she could not possibly risk a love affair with him.

"Do you really think that's possible, Cole? With all that stands between us?" she whispered.

His head snapped toward her, the gray gaze ruthlessly intent. "Nothing stands between us but your stubborn female curiosity and arrogance."

Kelsey drew back as if he'd slapped her. "Thank you, Mr. Stockton, for your succinct analysis of the situation!"

Cole said something explicit and savage. Then he appeared to take a tight rein on his temper. "Please, Kelsey. Just give us another chance, will you? Give us this week together. That's all I'm asking of you."

To have Cole Stockton asking—no, *pleading*—for such a favor was a distinctly unsettling shock, Kelsey discovered. It took away her breath for a timeless instant. She was a fool to allow him so close, an idiot even to listen to him. But she could not deny her emotional response. A week ago she would not have believed that Cole would resort to pleading for anything, let alone a woman's patience. Kelsey touched the tip of her tongue to her lower lip, her pulse picking up speed as she acknowledged the yearning inside her.

"Cole, if you would at least tell me about those payments Roger is making to you..." she began uncertainly, seeking some kind of compromise, any kind of compromise.

He closed his dark lashes, every line of his face unyielding. "It doesn't concern you, Kelsey. It's between Roger and me. Your stepfather wants it that way, and he trusts me to keep my word on the matter. I can't discuss it with you."

"I'll just have to trust you, is that it?" She sighed.

He lifted his lashes. "Is that too much to ask?"

"In all honesty, I think it is," she told him quietly. "But that's not going to stop you, is it? You're going to ask it, anyway."

He sat up on the lounger, reaching out to capture her hand in a compelling grip. Kelsey shivered under the stark intensity in him. She felt mesmerized beneath the force of the power he was wielding over her.

"Yes, I'm going to ask for your trust. I've told you

that I think it exists. I just want you to acknowledge it so we can build on it."

Wariness blazed in the depths of her eyes as she sat very still under his grasp. "And what are you prepared to give me in return, Cole?"

"Anything I can," he answered simply.

"Except the truth about you and your past," she concluded. *Or your love*, she added in painful silence. If Cole did not understand why she needed to know everything there was to know about him; if he didn't realize why she had pushed and prodded and tried to force open, honest communication between them, then he didn't understand anything at all about love. If he didn't comprehend it, he could not give it. There was no future for her with Cole Stockton.

"I have given you my word that I will never lie to you," he countered roughly.

"Oh, Cole," she breathed helplessly.

"Just give us a chance, honey. That's all I'm asking. I give you my word, I won't push you into bed this week. I only want to spend the time with you."

"It won't change anything," she tried to protest, hearing the uncertainty in her own words and cursing it. "Too much has already gone wrong between us...."

"That's in the past, Kelsey," he told her. "And I've learned how to put the past behind me."

"Just close a door and walk away?" she asked sadly.

"Whatever it takes," he said, shrugging.

"And you call *me* arrogant," she murmured, shaking her head in wonder.

"Kelsey?"

She sought for some rational, face-saving way out of

the dilemma. "The ship isn't that big," she tried crisply. "I can't very well spend the next week running from one end to the other just to avoid you, can I?"

His mouth crooked and the relief was plain in his eyes. "Is that a roundabout way of telling me you're not going to try to pretend I don't exist for the next few days?"

She looked at him gravely. "Cole, I might try to run from you, I might try to ignore you or I might try to strangle you, but I don't think I could ever pretend you don't exist!"

Kelsey heard the capitulation in her own words, and the flash of satisfaction in Cole's icicle eyes told her he had heard it, too.

"I'll show you how it's done, honey."

"How what's done?"

"How to close a door and start over."

"You're an expert?"

He brushed the question aside, lifting a hand in a negligent gesture that brought a steward hurrying over to the lounger.

"Another glass of iced tea, please," Cole ordered politely. "The ice in this one seems to have melted."

"Yes, sir." The steward started toward the poolside bar to put in the order.

"And speaking of melting ice," Cole began firmly, turning back to Kelsey.

"Were we speaking of it?"

"Oh, yes," he assured her gently. "We most certainly were."

Kelsey didn't miss his meaning. She fully understood he was referring to her. But privately she thought

he was wrong. True, she might have softened a little
this morning under the heat of his insistence, but it
seemed to her the real melting action had just taken
place in Cole's ice-colored eyes.

Her wary, very cautious agreement to spend the
week with him had raised the temperature in those
eyes by several degrees. She couldn't help speculating
on what her outright surrender would accomplish.

It was too bad that the risks remained so high. Because the urge to allow herself to love Cole Stockton
was a singing compulsion in her veins.

SIX

"That's Cibola coming up straight ahead." His voice raised so the passengers could hear him over the whine of the Cessna's engine, the pilot indicated a patch of gray-green looming above the ocean surface. "And that little cluster of shacks near the harbor is what passes for a village. The rest of the island is just about empty."

"Thank goodness we're almost there." Sitting in one of the rear seats of the four passenger plane, Kelsey's fervent comment went unheard by either the rather taciturn pilot or Cole, who was sitting in the right front seat.

They had left the airport on St. Thomas half an hour earlier, and as soon as the little plane had leaped skyward Kelsey had begun to question the decision to hire a small plane for the hop to Cibola. Actually, she had questioned the plan even before that. The moment she had seen the heavyset pilot with his mirrored sunglasses and his sweat-stained shirt she had wondered aloud about the wisdom of flying to Cibola.

"Would you prefer to swim?" Cole had inquired laconically.

"I don't like people who wear mirrored sunglasses," Kelsey had grumbled.

"You don't have to love the guy. All we need to worry about is whether he's qualified to fly a plane to that island where your genius lives."

Ray, the pilot, didn't appear to bother with the formality of a last name. He had been ready and waiting for them at the airport when Kelsey and Cole had arrived.

"Only supposed to be one of you," Ray had pointed out skeptically, eyeing Cole, who was carrying the attaché case.

"Plans have changed slightly," Cole had told him calmly. "Ready to leave?"

"Yeah, I reckon so."

Kelsey had told herself she could hardly criticize Ray for his sweat-dampened clothing. Her own yellow cotton safari-style shirt was clinging uncomfortably to her skin as she followed the pilot across the hot pavement. The heavy humidity combined with the heat of the day made it impossible to stay serenely cool. She wished she had worn a short skirt instead of the white jeans. It might have been more comfortable.

Cole didn't appear particularly affected by the muggy heat. Dressed in his customary khaki clothes and a pair of low leather boots, he had looked quite at ease in the tropical surroundings.

In fact, Kelsey told herself now, as she watched Cibola coming closer on the horizon, one could even say Cole looked almost at home.

She'd had plenty of time to speculate on Cole's behavior during the past twenty-four hours. The noise of the Cessna engines had made conversation a strain. So she had sat quietly in the rear seat and reflected on the wary relationship she had allowed herself to enter.

Not that she'd had much choice in the basic decision, she decided wryly. It was either compromise with Cole or try to escape the ship. It hadn't taken any great degree of intelligence to reason that much out. Cole was on board with only one purpose in mind, and that was to force her back into a relationship on his terms. Kelsey was learning the hard way that when he set himself a goal he allowed nothing to get in his path.

She had surrendered at least partially, Kelsey knew, but she had been prepared for the whole fragile situation to collapse under the weight of the first major confrontation. And she had assumed that confrontation would take place at her stateroom door last night.

Cole had made no secret of his desire during the evening they had spent together. But he'd behaved as the polite, quietly restrained escort he had been on the weekends this past month. By the time she had eaten dinner with him, attended the cabaret show and then danced with him out on deck under the stars, she had finally begun to relax.

No, Kelsey told herself with rigorous honesty, she had more than relaxed. She had begun to slip back under the spell of the man. It had done no good to remind herself what had happened the last time she had attempted to break free of that emotional sorcery. She had still found herself going willingly into his arms as they danced, her tawny head on his shoulder and her body luxuriating in the feel of his hands on her waist.

When the moment had come, as she had known it would, and they found themselves standing in the hall outside her stateroom door, only her hard-won caution had prevented her from surrendering completely to the magic and the man.

"Kelsey?" There had been a hungry question in the way Cole had said her name as he feathered a kiss along the line of her throat. And demand had been buried just beneath the question.

"No," she had managed starkly, focusing on the first button of his dark, formal shirt. Her crimson-tipped nails had flexed unconsciously into the black fabric of his jacket sleeve. She had been violently aware of the tension in him, and for a precarious instant she wondered if he would explode the way he had that fateful night in her mother's home.

"Kelsey, honey, I'll make it good for you. I'll make you forget the fear and the caution and all the questions."

Kelsey had shivered under the rough honey of his words and the sensual glide of his fingers as he stroked the nape of her neck. He had felt that telltale tremor. She had known he felt it, because she had immediately sensed the leaping satisfaction in him. Perhaps it had been that knowledge that had given her the fortitude to stand by her decision.

"No," she had said again, very softly but very firmly.

He had hesitated then, and she had felt the strength in his hands as he tightened them ever so slightly on the curve of her shoulder. But Cole had nodded, as if to himself, and stepped back, gray eyes as unreadable as fog.

"Good night, Kelsey. I'll pick you up for breakfast."

She had stood in the corridor and watched him walk away. He hadn't looked back.

Now Kelsey sat watching the approach of Valentine's island, and told herself for what must have been the thousandth time that she had made the right decision last night. She had known from the beginning that Cole Stockton was fire and that she was in danger of being consumed by the blaze. She must stay just out of reach for her own safety. There was no doubt that the intricate dance at the edge of the flames was a dangerous one.

Ray made a competent landing on the small dirt strip that had been hacked into the leeward side of the tiny island. He taxied to the far end and shut down the engines. The strip paralleled the rocky shoreline. As far as Kelsey could see the only respectable patch of sandy beach was that lying in a crescent framing a small bay not far away. It was protected by a rock-strewn, craggy cliff.

"I don't see anyone waiting for us," Kelsey said, peering through the window at the heavy foliage that began at the edge of the dirt strip and climbed back to the hills forming a backbone down the long, narrow island.

"That's not my problem," Ray noted. "How long you want me to wait?"

"We'll give the guy half an hour to show," Cole said

decisively, unlatching his door to let some breeze into the cabin of the plane.

Kelsey frowned. "I can't leave until I've delivered that case."

"Time on the ground is the same price as time in the air," Ray reminded them curtly.

"Half an hour," Cole repeated. He stepped easily out of the Cessna and then turned to help Kelsey.

"Cole, I have a job to do. I can't leave until that case has been turned over to Valentine."

"'Valentine'?" Ray interrupted. "The weirdo who messes around with computers?"

"That's right," Kelsey replied quickly, glancing back into the plane where Ray still sat. "Do you know him?"

"I've brought other deliveries to him." Ray nodded. "He's got a shack up in those hills. Not too far. He usually walks down to meet the plane."

"Maybe he forgot this was the day I'm supposed to arrive," Kelsey said thoughtfully.

"Honey," Cole said, "on an island this small he's bound to have heard the Cessna coming in for a landing. Even if he did forget the date, he probably remembered as soon as he heard the plane. He'll be down soon. If he's coming at all."

Kelsey was beginning to realize just how completely Cole was taking over. On an hour-by-hour basis the number of little decisions he made for her was growing. Last night most of the decisions had been disguised as suggestions, she acknowledged. Still, she had wound up with the Cabernet wine he had brought to her attention and the scallops in basil sauce he had mentioned at dinner. Later he had begun ordering her drinks without consulting her. This morning he had organized the trip from the ship into Charlotte Amalie, the port town. It was Cole who had commandeered a taxi to the airport and located the one-man charter service run by Ray.

It was true that all his actions had been very helpful, Kelsey thought, but Cole's helpfulness was beginning to turn into something more direct. Now he was starting to decide how she should handle her business on Cibola. It was time to remind him she was still in charge of herself and her task.

"We'll give him fifteen minutes," she declared calmly. "And then we'll go check his house."

Cole slanted her a strange look, as if deciding how to deal with Kelsey's deliberate assertiveness. She had the impression he was on the verge of issuing a clear-cut command, and then he appeared to think better of the idea.

"Kelsey, believe me, if he's anywhere in the vicinity, he'll have heard the plane arrive. If he doesn't come down it must be because he's not particularly interested in the printouts. I don't think we ought to track him down. You've told me, yourself, the guy's a little strange."

"Fifteen minutes and then we'll go check his place," Kelsey repeated firmly. She pretended to ignore the flash of irritation that came and went in Cole's expression. Whatever he had done in his past, she decided, he had been accustomed to being in command.

One more tiny little clue to his background. As if there were any point in collecting such tidbits, she reminded herself sadly. Cole was not likely ever to fit the pieces of the puzzle together for her.

"We'll see," he temporized.

But fifteen minutes later Kelsey decided to act. The thick heat was making her think longingly of the air conditioning on board the ship. She stood up from where she had been sitting on the attaché case under the shadow of the Cessna wing and announced the next step.

"Come on, Cole. Let's go see if we can find him."

Cole, who had been hunkered down on his heels beside her, got slowly to his feet, frowning. "Kelsey, I really don't think he's around."

"I have to make certain. Walt is going to be very upset if I don't deliver this case."

"And Walt's getting upset matters?" Cole inquired wryly.

"Of course it does. He's my boss!"

"The road up to Valentine's shack starts over there," Ray offered. He was sitting in the Cessna, clearly bored by the entire matter. "How long do you want me to give you?"

"How long will it take to walk there?" Kelsey asked.

"No more than ten minutes."

Cole took over, speaking coldly. "You'll wait until we get back," he told the pilot. "Regardless of how long it takes. Don't worry, you'll be paid. All right, Kelsey. If you're dead set on this, let's get going." He picked up the attaché case and started in the direction Ray had indicated.

Kelsey followed quickly, stepping out from the shelter of the wing and into the full heat of the day. "This climate is awfully humid. I don't think I'd like to live in the tropics."

"You get used to it," Cole said absently.

"It doesn't seem to bother you," Kelsey noted, unable to resist the delicate probe.

"Stop fishing for information, honey," Cole retorted dryly. "Save your breath for the walk up to Valentine's place. You're going to need it."

You'd think I'd learn, Kelsey thought grimly. Then she decided to take Cole's advice. The walk through the thickening foliage required an effort. For one thing, the path they were following hardly constituted a "road," Kelsey decided. Ray had been generous labeling the narrow dirt track as such. It was overgrown with a variety of unidentifiable greenery and it had obviously never been used by a vehicle larger than a motorbike. It climbed quite steeply up into the hills and with every step the surrounding plant life seemed to grow heavier."

"This is turning into a real jungle," Kelsey observed.

"I don't like this," Cole said quietly, coming to a complete halt in the middle of the track. "I don't see any signs of Valentine's shack and I just don't like the feel of the place."

"Well, I'm not exactly enjoying this little afternoon stroll, either," she tossed back irritably. "If you want to go wait with Ray, feel free."

"Don't be an idiot," Cole growled. "Do you really think I'd go back to the plane and leave you to continue this crazy hike by yourself?"

Kelsey looked up at him through lowered lashes. "Uh, no."

Cole abandon her at this juncture? Impossible. He would no more leave her alone in this overgrown garden than he would fly. Kelsey knew that with such certainty that it seemed ludicrous even to question it. Cole was right, she thought uneasily. In some ways she did know him and trust him. It made no sense, but she couldn't deny the facts.

"I don't like anything about this job you've got," Cole went on darkly as he turned to continue along the path. "But what I like least is that Gladwin would send you on a stupid task like this one just to save himself a few bucks in professional-courier fees."

"I offered to do it! He didn't force me." Kelsey defended her boss automatically.

"But it was his idea."

"So what? It was a perfectly reasonable idea."

"'Reasonable'? To send a woman alone into a jungle like this?" Cole demanded almost fiercely.

"Walt's never actually been to Cibola himself. He had no way of knowing it was quite this primitive. Sitting in an office in San Jose, Cibola sounds very appealing. A picturesque tropical paradise," Kelsey informed him frostily.

Again Cole halted, swinging around with an abrupt decisiveness that took Kelsey by surprise. His face was set in implacable lines. "This is far enough, Kelsey. We're on a fool's errand. Turn around and start back toward the airstrip."

Kelsey almost found herself obeying without question. Cole wasn't making a suggestion; he was issuing an order, and in a manner that elicited instinctive compliance. If she hadn't been trying to fight him on one level or another for the past week, she probably would have followed orders. As it was, it took an astonishing amount of willpower to dig in her heels.

"Cole, I came here to do a job. I'm not going back until I've given it my best—"

The sudden revving of an aircraft engine shattered the silence.

"Damn it to hell." Cole uttered the oath with weary resignation rather than any real heat.

"What's going on?" Kelsey turned to gaze back toward the landing strip, but she could see nothing through the foliage. "Is that the Cessna?"

"I'm afraid so." Cole was looking up toward the sky now, and Kelsey followed his gaze. The Cessna was already several hundred feet in the air, heading back in the direction from which it had come.

"He's leaving! Ray's leaving us here!" she gasped. "He can't do that. How will we get back to the ship?"

"An excellent question," Cole said dryly.

"But why would he leave us behind?" Kelsey looked up at him in total bewilderment.

"I think our old friend Ray conducts business on a very straightforward version of the free-enterprise principle," Cole murmured thoughtfully. "In other words, he'll work for whoever pays him the most. Just on a hunch I'd guess someone paid him more to leave us here than he was paid to take us back to the ship."

"But why would anyone want to...oh, my God." Kelsey's eyes opened very wide as she glanced at the black attaché case Cole was holding. "You don't really think someone would go to these lengths to get hold of those, do you?" she asked weakly.

"Kelsey, the more I get to know about your job and your boss, the less I like either."

"I don't see why you have to drag Walt into this," she snapped, thoroughly annoyed. "It's hardly his fault."

"Well, if it makes you feel any better, I can't find anything particularly wonderful to say about myself right now, either. I must have been out of my mind to let you go through with your plans to deliver these papers. I should have listened to my head instead of my, uh, hormones. Come on, let's get moving." He started back up the path with a swift, ground-eating stride.

"But, Cole...!" Kelsey found herself hurrying to keep up with him. The stylish yellow safari shirt was clinging to her damp skin in earnest now as Cole's pace forced her to exert herself in the heat. "Why go any farther in this direction? Shouldn't we go back to the airstrip? Maybe someone else will come along. Or there's that little fishing village on the other side of the island. The one Ray mentioned. Maybe we should head for it."

"Those are probably the two directions we'll be expected to head. So I think we'll skip both," Cole tossed back over his shoulder.

Kelsey stared at his back as he continued to forge easily ahead on the trail. "What do you mean by that? Cole, do you actually think someone might be waiting for us down at that landing strip?" It was taking a while for the reality of the situation to sink in, Kelsey realized, slightly dazed. She couldn't yet quite believe all the frightening implications of the fact that Ray had abandoned them.

Cole, on the other hand, seemed to have accepted the worst possibilities with hardly a flicker of an eyelash. As if he had been half expecting this bizarre turn of events.

"I think it's very likely someone will be watching for us to dash back to the strip. It's what most people would instinctively do if their transportation had just disappeared. And once out in the open we'd be a couple of sitting ducks."

"You're certainly adjusting to the situation with remarkable ease," Kelsey gritted caustically. "None of this seems to have fazed you in the least."

"Save your breath, Kelsey," he advised laconically. "You're going to need it. This trail is getting steeper."

Kelsey bit back a sharp retort, aware that he was right. The patch was climbing rapidly now, and the pace Cole was setting, combined with the oppressive heat, was taking a lot out of her.

So Kelsey stopped flinging questions and comments at Cole's impervious back and started thinking, instead. And the first thing that occurred to her was that the bottom line so far contained a very simple entry.

Simple and alarming. Cole had the attaché case and she was alone with Cole.

Kelsey caught her breath as she finally put the facts together. Cole had known all about this side trip. He'd known she'd be taking the case full of printouts to the mysterious Valentine. He had examined the contents of the attaché case and then he'd calmly removed the case from her room. And it had been Cole who had located Ray back in St. Thomas. Now it was Cole who was leading her deeper into the island jungle.

Kelsey came to a halt in the middle of the trail.

Ahead of her, Cole sensed at once that she had stopped. He turned back, annoyed at having to deal with more questions when he was trying to think his way through the mess.

"Kelsey?" he growled. Perhaps she was exhausted already. This heat could get to someone who wasn't acclimated. It was even beginning to affect him, although he'd had all those years in one steaming hellhole after another to get used to it. One year of civilized living in Carmel had been sufficient to undo a fair amount of conditioning, he decided wryly. "Kelsey, I know it's hot and you're getting tired, but we have to keep going."

"Do we?" she asked with a distant politeness that finally told him what the problem was. "Who says we have to keep going, Cole?"

He felt a shaft of cold anguish as he realized what was going through her head. Then he flicked an assessing gaze over her, noting the way the yellow shirt was outlining the curve of her breasts as she inhaled deeply to catch her breath. Her tawny hair was no longer a neat, sophisticated frame for her face, now perspiration-dampened. Instead it was beginning to get tangled from too many brushes against the persistent greenery along the path. The snug-fitting white jeans were rapidly becoming dirty, and when she wiped her forehead with the back of her hand she left a small smudge. She glared at him with wary, defiant eyes, her slender body poised and tense.

"You know," Cole said with perfect honesty. "For

some reason that utterly defeats me, you look as sexy as hell."

The off-the-wall remark startled her, as he had intended it should. While it was nothing less than the truth, because she always looked sexy to him, he had said the words aloud as a way of breaking through the fear he saw in her eyes.

"This is not a joke, damn it. Tell me what's going on!"

Better to have her angry than fearful, Cole decided. "How should I know what's going on? You're the one who insisted on coming to this island."

"You're the one who insisted on coming with me." Her eyes darted downward toward the black case. "And you're the one who has his hands on those printouts."

Cole felt himself tighten under the uncertainty and accusation he saw in her eyes. "You haven't got much choice, Kelsey," he told her brutally. "You're going to have to trust me."

"You've been saying that in one way or another since the day we met. And like an idiot, I keep letting you talk me into giving you one more chance. Now I find myself stranded on a lonely island in the middle of the Caribbean with you and that attaché case."

"The problem is that I can't be sure just how lonely we really are," he explained coldly. "For you this is going to be a clear-cut case of 'better the devil you know than the one you don't.' Your Mr. Valentine is still floating around out here someplace and Lord knows who else. It's a safe bet we're not completely alone on this island. Someone must want the printouts, and whoever it is won't be satisfied until he has the case."

"How do I know you aren't that someone?" she flared.

"Trust me," he grated, and started back up the path.

"Damn you, Cole Stockton! You've told me to trust you one too many times! You may be good at giving orders, but I am not so good at taking them blindly. In any case, trust is the one thing you can't force someone to give. I want answers, Cole. And I want them now."

Cole considered his options. There weren't very many. He was going to have to handle this as ruthlessly and efficiently as possible. For all he knew her life depended on his getting her completely under his control. When it came to protecting her he'd do whatever had to be done.

The decision made, he followed through on it the way he always did on his decisions. It was one of the old habits that he'd probably never completely shake. Survival had never favored those who vacillated over their decisions.

He saw the shock that replaced the anger and uncertainty in Kelsey's hazel eyes as he moved toward her with flowing speed. She never even had a chance to run. Cole closed his fingers over her shoulder, letting her feel the weight of his strength. Then he hauled her very close, trapping her startled gaze.

"I don't have any answers for you, Kelsey." Deliberately he threw all the hard intimidation he had at his command into the words. He had to break her stubborn will to resist, and do it quickly. "No answers, but I do have a few observations. I'll give it to you short and sweet. We are in a very unpleasant situation. Potentially dangerous. You are not equipped to get either of us out of this mess. Therefore you will have to rely on me, whether you fully trust me or not. *You have no choice, Kelsey.* Do you understand? Absolutely no choice. You will do as I tell you, no questions asked, and you will do it when I tell you. You will do it as quickly and as obediently as you can, because if you don't you will find I won't hesitate to do whatever it takes to enforce my orders. And I will give you fair warning, Kelsey. I am not at my most thoughtful and charming when I'm in a situation like this. In fact, I am a complete bastard. If you can't trust me in any other way, you'd better believe in that much. Now move on up that trail or I will drag you up it."

He stepped away from her, letting her see the absolute confidence he had in his own authority. Only he realized that the intimidation tactic wasn't going to work unless she genuinely feared or trusted him on some deep level.

When she slanted him a seething glance and then turned to stride ahead of him up the trail, Cole was left to ponder the inevitable question he had posed for himself. He could not be certain if it was fear or trust motivating her to obey. He could hope that it was trust, pray that it was trust. But he could not be certain.

It didn't matter, Cole told himself as he moved to follow Kelsey. As long as she obeyed him when the crunch came, it really didn't matter why she did it. But he knew he was lying to himself.

Ahead of him on the path, Kelsey was furiously trying to assess her own behavior and that of the man behind her. She could not fully explain why she had backed down so readily under the force of Cole's intimidation. She was, she acknowledged uneasily, a little afraid of him. When he claimed he could be a bastard in certain circumstances—dangerous circumstances—she believed him.

There was an underlying ruthlessness in Cole Stockton, Kelsey realized. She'd known that since the traumatic night he had taken her to bed. There was also an innate self-confidence and authority that he wore like a cloak. He was accustomed to being in command, both of himself and others.

Oh, yes. She believe him when he told her he could be a bastard. But that was about all she could realistically believe in, she cautioned herself. As usual around Cole, there were a lot more questions than answers. For the moment she would obey him. But she couldn't say why.

Perhaps it was simply that she had no choice.

Because she was in the lead, it was Kelsey who first saw the odd octagonal house in the jungle clearing. She slid to a halt, and Cole, who was only a step behind her, reached out to grasp her arm.

"That's far enough," he muttered, sweeping the cleared area with eyes that missed nothing.

"Valentine's place do you think?" Kelsey peered at the roughly hewn wooden house. She rather liked the strange octagonal design. The rooms would probably be pie shaped, she thought fleetingly. There were windows on all eight sides, and a heavy-duty generator was housed at the rear. There was no sign of a huge man with a long beard and wire-rimmed glasses.

"Must be," Cole said quietly. "You wait here. I'm going to have a look."

"I'll come with you," she began automatically, not particularly wanting to stay behind in the dense jungle when something as civilized as a house was beckoning.

"You'll stay here. And hang on to this." Cole thrust the attaché case into her hands. "Give me ten minutes."

"But, Cole—" Kelsey broke off at once as he switched a hard-eyed gaze at her. "All right," she muttered. "I'll stay here."

"You're learning," Cole grunted. He started to slip away into the nearby foliage but stopped when he felt Kelsey's fingers touch his sleeve.

"Cole, be careful," she heard herself whisper.

He looked startled, and then he briefly touched her fingers as they clung to his khaki shirt. "Yes," he agreed. She thought he was going to say something else, and then she decided he must have changed his mind.

He slipped away, and a few seconds later he had disappeared into the jungle. Kelsey stayed very still, holding the attaché case and thinking how easy it was for Cole to fade into the jungle.

When Cole reappeared a few moments later he was emerging from the dense growth on the opposite side of the clearing. She watched anxiously as he stepped out of the protective cover around him and calmly entered the house through a door that stood open. Kelsey held her breath until he materialized again in the doorway. Then he moved quickly back across the open ground and into the underbrush. A short time later she whirled, startled to see him suddenly appear beside her.

"You move like a ghost," she accused softly.

"And you look like you've just seen one. It's okay, honey. The place is empty."

"No sign of Valentine?"

Cole shook his head. "No, but someone has recently been through that place with a fine-tooth comb. It's been torn apart. Somebody was looking for something." He glanced down at the attaché case. "My guess is he didn't find it."

"What about Valentine? He wouldn't have torn his own house apart."

"Your guess is as good as mine. We're not going to stick around and see if he shows up, however. It's going to start getting dark in another hour or so. We're going to have to find someplace to spend the night."

"Couldn't we stay in Valentine's house?" Kelsey asked wistfully. But even as she asked the question she knew the answer. Cole had already decided they wouldn't be using the obvious source of shelter, and although she was putting up a brief argument about it, Kelsey also knew she would abide by his decision.

"Anyone who knows we're stranded on this side of the island will also know that this place is standing here like an open invitation."

"And you don't accept open invitations?" she hazarded.

"Only from you," he returned without any hesitation. "But I don't get many of those from you, do I?"

Kelsey would not have believed that in her bedraggled, perspiration-soaked, anxious state she could be capable of turning a rather vivid shade of red. "You don't usually bother to wait for them!"

Cole picked up the attaché case. "We're wasting time. Let's go."

Swallowing her protests, Kelsey obediently fell into step behind Cole. He led her off the trail and straight into the heavy undergrowth. The going was rough, and she had to fight to keep up the pace he set. But Kelsey didn't bother with complaints. There was no point, she decided realistically. Cole was not deliberately punishing her, he was simply doing what had to be done in order to find shelter before nightfall.

It occurred to Kelsey to question her growing confidence in Cole, but she was much too tired now to pursue that line of thought. She was lost as soon as they left the trail, vaguely aware only that they were heading downhill. Blindly she followed Cole, concentrating on the task of keeping up with him.

When they at last broke out into the open again it was at a point some distance from the airstrip. Across the wide, rocky beach the foaming water beckoned invitingly.

"What I wouldn't give for a swim right now," Kelsey murmured, eyeing the gentle waves wistfully. Eagerly she started forward, thinking she could at least get her feet wet.

"Later," Cole ordered softly. He reached out and unceremoniously yanked her back.

"Must you be so heavy-handed about everything?" she snapped, massaging her shoulder as she glared up at him. He wasn't looking at her, though. He seemed to be listening.

"At times like this, yes," he answered almost absently. "I tend to get heavy-handed when complications arise. And we've got another one."

"Another complication?" She stared up at him, perplexed.

"That's right."

"Now what?"

"Someone followed us down the hill, Kelsey."

"'Followed us'? Oh, my God!" She twirled, trying to peer into the jungle behind her, but it was impossible to see more than a few feet. "Where is he?"

"Several yards back. He stopped when we did. Probably waiting to see what we'll do next."

"What *are* we going to do next?" she asked evenly.

"Make our visitor welcome, of course." He caught her wrist and led her along the edge of the beach.

At no point did they actually step out into the open. Cole hugged the cover of the undergrowth with a skill that Kelsey knew had come with years of practice. Pulling her along in his wake, he somehow managed to assure her of cover, too.

The rocky beach grew into a cliff that rose a short distance above the surf. Huge chunks of stone littered the landscape from the edge of the jungle to the sea's edge. Cole wove a path between the boulders until he seemed to find what he was looking for.

"This will have to do. Down you go, Kelsey, and stay there until I tell you to get up. Clear?" He urged her behind a pile of tumbled boulders, using his weight to push her down to a crouching position. When she glanced up at him she shivered at the sight of the lethal expression that carved his features.

"Cole?"

"Just stay put, Kelsey." He handed over the attaché case again, and then he seemed to melt into the landscape, losing himself amid the heavy stone shapes that surrounded him.

Kelsey watched him go and realized she was suddenly very afraid. And her fear was not of Cole. Rather, she admitted silently, it was for him. The thought of anything happening to him in that jungle filled her with a dread that had nothing to do with her own situation.

It was then that Kelsey began to realize how inevitably committed she was becoming to Cole Stockton. In spite of the fact that she knew almost nothing about him and in spite of her suspicions that whatever had shaped his past had not been particularly civilized, her own fate was now inextricably bound up with his. She waited alone behind the shelter of the stone, and knew how her female ancestors had felt when they waited in caves for the return of their men from the hunt.

SEVEN

He was a giant of a man, but it wasn't his size that made him dangerous, Cole knew. It was the way he moved like a cat through the jungle.

A rather out-of-practice cat, Cole conceded as he tracked his quarry. The big man wasn't quite as silent or as careful as he should have been, but Cole was willing to bet that at one time Valentine had been very skilled, indeed.

It had to be Valentine. From the brief glimpses he got as he circled around behind the man, Cole decided no one else could fit the description Kelsey had been given. Huge, a long beard and gold wire-rimmed glasses.

No one had apparently bothered to tell Kelsey that the man called "Valentine" had once done something far more lethal than program computers. Perhaps no one had realized it.

But as soon as he'd become aware of being followed, Cole had understood one or two crucial facts about their pursuer. The first was that he was a trained hunter and the second was that the game Valentine had once been taught to hunt was probably the two-legged variety.

It takes one to know one, Cole thought grimly as he closed in behind the massive Valentine. He could only hope that the big man's skills might have grown a shade rustier than his own.

Silently he glided to a point a few feet behind the bearded man. Balanced lightly, feet spread slightly apart, Cole collected himself physically and then called out softly.

"Valentine's Day is going to be a little late this year."

The huge man spun around, and Cole found himself being rapidly scrutinized and assessed by a pair of very perceptive blue eyes. For a moment the two men stood poised, confronting each other across the short distance.

"I don't know whether or not Valentine's Day is going to be late this year, but I surely do know that today hasn't been it. Just one damned thing after another. And now you." Valentine's voice was a low, bearlike growl. Perfectly suited to the man.

"And now me," Cole agreed laconically. "If it makes you feel any better, today hasn't exactly been one of my red-letter days, either."

"You're with the woman." It was a statement, not a question.

"Yeah, I'm with the woman."

"Do you mind telling me in what capacity?" Valentine flexed his big hands a little, as if they were stiff.

Cole noted the small movement, and his mouth twisted into a faint smile. He instinctively checked his own balance and decided it was as good as it was going to get. It had been a long time, and nothing stayed well honed if a man didn't practice frequently.

"You could say I'm looking after her," he explained very politely to Valentine.

"Protection, hmm. Paid or unpaid?"

"I look after her because she belongs to me," Cole said with deadly simplicity.

At once Valentine seemed to relax. "That," he rumbled gently, "explains a few things. Not everything, but a few things. I think, sir, that we may be on the same side."

"And what side would that be?" Cole felt the tension lessening, but he didn't change his balanced stance.

"Opposite from the one those two jokers who tore up my place are on." Valentine absently fingered his beard, but his piercing blue eyes continued to peer perceptively through the wire-rimmed glasses. "Like I said, it hasn't exactly been Valentine's Day around here."

"Two of them?"

Valentine nodded. "And armed."

"Unlike us," Cole said wearily.

"Unlike us," Valentine agreed.

"It's going to be a long day. I suppose I'd better introduce you to the lady who came all this way to see you."

"Your lady," Valentine clarified.

"Mine. Although I'm not sure she knows it yet." He motioned slightly with one hand. "After you."

Valentine arched a shaggy brow, mild amusement flickering behind the lenses of his glasses. "Cautious sort, aren't you?" He swung around and started to make his way toward the rocky beach.

"These days I prefer to think of myself as just well mannered, not cautious." Cole fell into step behind Valentine.

"Do you succeed in fooling yourself?"

"Sometimes," Cole said. "How about you?"

"Sometimes I get lucky and fool myself, too," Valentine said very softly.

"I guess we're a pair of real con artists. Out to deceive the toughest audience in the world—ourselves."

"I think," Valentine said slowly, glancing back over his broad shoulder, "that being con artists is probably better than what we were before."

The two men exchanged a look of masculine understanding that spoke volumes. And then Cole shrugged. "That's what I keep telling myself."

"Where did you hide your lady?" Valentine asked curiously as he emerged from the undergrowth and stood scanning the boulder-strewn landscape.

"Valentine!" Kelsey, who had been watching the edge of the jungle for any sign of Cole's return, leaped to her feet and came racing toward the two men. "You must be Valentine." She grinned, liking the big man on sight. "I'm so glad it was you following us. I've been worried sick, wondering what Cole was doing charging around in that overgrown weed garden. Are you okay? Cole said your house was ransacked. What's going on here, anyway?"

Valentine's white teeth flashed through his beard, and Kelsey decided that any resemblance the man might have had to Santa Claus ended with that smile.

The thick beard could not hide the hint of a hunting wolf gleaming within the grin. In that moment she realized the expression reminded her rather forcibly of Cole's rare smiles.

Two of a kind. The thought went through her head in a burst of intuition that she immediately discounted. What a ridiculous notion. Valentine and Cole were as different as night and day. One was a big, bearded, eccentric computer genius. The other was a reclusive, frustratingly uncommunicative, arrogant businessman. But her female intuition was telling her something else.

"I'm fine. You must be Miss Murdock. Sorry about the change of plans around here. I assure you, it wasn't my idea. Just as well you brought your friend here along."

Kelsey wrinkled her nose at Cole. "I didn't have much choice. Cole insisted on coming with me."

"'Cole'?" Valentine asked blandly.

"Haven't the two of you introduced yourselves? Valentine, this is Cole Stockton." Kelsey glared from one to the other.

"Oh, we introduced ourselves," Cole drawled. "We just didn't get around to exchanging names." He nodded formally to Valentine.

"My pleasure," Valentine murmured.

Kelsey was aware of the cryptic overtones in the air, but she couldn't understand them. It was as if Valentine and Cole knew far more about each other than either let on, and yet she knew neither had met until a few minutes ago.

"So much for life's little pleasantries," Cole said

smoothly. "I suggest we get on with a few of its necessities. In case no one else has noticed, it's starting to get dark. This is your territory, Valentine. Any suggestions of where we might stash Kelsey for the night?"

"'Stash' me!" she echoed, astonished. "What's that supposed to mean?"

"It means hide you," Cole explained, as if to a child.

"What about you two?" she demanded, not liking the direction of the conversation.

"Your man and I have a little business to take care of, Miss Murdock," Valentine said gently. "There are a couple of other folks on this side of the island. Not your average tourists, I'm afraid."

"The people who ransacked your house? Who are they, Valentine? Are they after these printouts?" Kelsey tapped the attaché case with the toe of her sandal.

"That's the theory I'm going on at the moment. Come on, Kelsey, I'll show you and your man a nice, safe spot."

Kelsey flushed, darting a quick glance at Cole, who was already moving to take her arm and guide her in Valentine's wake. "He's not 'my man,'" she felt obliged to mumble. "His name is Cole."

Valentine and Cole both ignored the remark. Cole's face was set in hard lines as he steered Kelsey after the other man. She felt a little awkward around these two, Kelsey decided resentfully. Both of them moved with that silent, graceful stride she had always found unnerving in Cole.

"You two didn't happen to be ballet dancers sometime in your past, did you?" she muttered at one point as Cole kept her from tripping over a tree root. As the sun set on the other side of the hills that divided the island, night descended quickly. It was getting difficult to see.

Valentine chuckled softly up ahead in the gathering shadows.

"Don't pay any attention to her," Cole advised. "She's addicted to the game of twenty questions."

"And you don't like to play it with her, right?" Valentine asked with what sounded like complete understanding.

"Not when the questions always center around ancient history," Cole murmured.

"You want some current questions?" Kelsey gritted, infuriated at the way the two men were discussing her. "I'll give you a couple. Number one, what are you two planning to do tonight? And where are those two people who went through your house, Valentine? What exactly happened here today?"

"Actually," Cole interrupted mildly, "I'm a little curious on that subject myself, Valentine."

"I'll tell you everything I know, which I'm afraid isn't much, as soon as we get to the cave."

"A 'cave'?" Kelsey considered that. "I hate caves. They give me the willies."

"If this cave solves the problem of keeping you safely hidden tonight, then you will learn to tolerate the 'willies,'" Cole informed her bluntly.

"One of these days," Kelsey retorted seethingly, "we're going to have a long talk about your infuriating arrogance!"

"But not tonight," he said.

Kelsey remained silent for the rest of the hurried

hike to the cave Valentine had selected. As soon as she saw it buried in the shadows of a cliff face, Kelsey knew she was going to hate every moment spent inside its dark mouth. But there was no doubt about the degree of security it offered. Heavy foliage concealed the entrance until one was virtually in front of it. It faced toward the ocean, but no one standing out on the rocky beach would have noticed it unless he knew exactly where to look. She couldn't deny it would serve as an excellent hiding place. With a giant effort of will she managed to conceal her shudder as Valentine led her and Cole inside.

"What about bats?" she asked suddenly.

"There aren't any," Valentine assured her.

"Rats?"

"The only kind of rats we have to worry about tonight are the two-legged variety," Cole told her as the three of them stood in the mouth of the cave and surveyed it in the fading light.

"Snakes?"

"A few lizards," Valentine said reassuringly. "That's all. There's even a nice, freshwater spring near the entrance. Have a seat, both of you. Welcome to my vacation cottage." He indicated a couple of large rocks off to one side.

"Lizards, huh?" Kelsey glanced around skeptically. "And I'm supposed to wait here while you guys go off to see what's happening?"

Cole and Valentine exchanged glances. "Something like that," Cole agreed dryly. "Let's hear your story, Valentine. What did go on today?"

Valentine sank down onto a rock, shaking his

shaggy head. "Beats me. I've been trying to put two and two together, and the only thing I can come up with is that someone wants those printouts. There are a heck of a lot of unknowns. All I do know for certain is that I left the house at dawn for my usual run on the beach. I was about halfway through my normal course, when I spotted a launch moving very quietly into that small bay near the landing strip. Two unsavory types came ashore and the third took off in the launch. Presumably he'll be returning at a prearranged time."

"What did you do?" Kelsey asked.

Valentine lifted one massive shoulder. "Being of a basically inquisitive nature, I followed the two gentlemen who came ashore. It didn't take long before I realized they were heading for my place. I got there just as they were about to go inside. I thought about doing something dramatic at that point, and then I decided to give the situation a little time. For one thing, I knew you were due later on today, Kelsey, and I didn't think Flex-Glad would appreciate my letting one of their lady administrative types walk into an awkward situation like this. Especially not when she was carrying some important printouts." Valentine broke off to smile meaningfully. "Of course, I didn't know you'd be bringing along your own protection."

"The printouts are the only things our two visitors could possibly want?" Cole asked quietly. "No chance this isn't something, uh, personal?"

"Cole, what a crazy question!" Kelsey gasped. "How could it be personal? Who would want to hurt Valentine? He lives all alone and bothers absolutely no one."

Valentine grinned. "Just your average, lovable island eccentric who asks nothing more out of life than to be left alone with his computer."

"And who happens to be a con artist," Cole tossed back smoothly.

"Takes one to know one," Valentine quoted.

"What on earth are you two talking about?" Kelsey burst in, thoroughly annoyed. She swung accusing glances from one to the other.

Valentine's derisive grin faded. "Nothing, Kelsey. Just a private joke."

"The two of you have hardly known each other long enough to have developed a repertoire of private jokes!"

"You're absolutely right," Cole said firmly. "So let's get back to business. You're sure the printouts are the problem here?"

Valentine nodded, sobering completely. "I'm sure, Stockton. The analysis of the theoretical data I've been working on could give someone a real jump ahead in the fast lane of artificial intelligence. I've been approaching some fundamental problems from an entirely new direction. Hate to sound so immodest, but the truth is, that stuff in the attaché case is worth someone's while to go after. Besides, none of this bears the marks of any unsettled personal business. I don't know those two jokers. Furthermore, after they finished demolishing the inside of my home and went their merry way, I had a look to see if I could tell what they'd been searching for. Everything near the computer, including all my hardcopy files had been torn apart. I decided to remove a certain personal possession I value highly and vacate the premises temporarily. Thought it might be interesting to wait and see what happened. The two from the boat blundered around for a while trying to find me. By now I think they've assumed I must be over in the village. I watched them go down the hill to wait for the plane."

"How would they know what to look for if they are after this artificial-intelligence data?" Kelsey asked.

"Not a bad question," Cole said, sounding mildly surprised. "I had a look at that stuff in the attaché case, Valentine. If I hadn't known it was important enough for someone to keep under lock and key, I would never have been able to guess. It would take an expert to identify those printouts as valuable."

"Not if they'd been instructed to look for the alpha numeric code on each page. Gladwin and I worked it out back at the beginning to keep the data from getting mixed up with other kinds of material."

"Would they have known I was bringing the data today?" Kelsey wondered.

"I'd say it's obvious they did," Cole offered. "Someone had to bribe good old Ray to take off without us."

"I heard the plane leaving," Valentine said. "I'm afraid good old Ray will do anything for a buck."

"Why did you follow us, Valentine? Why not just show yourself when we arrived at your place?" Kelsey fixed him with a curious glance.

"Because he wasn't sure where I fitted into the picture," Cole explained for the other man.

"But now I know," Valentine murmured.

"You two certainly seem to have arrived at a fair degree of mutual understanding during that short introduction in the woods," Kelsey complained. What was it with these two men, she wondered.

"We ex-ballet dancers recognize each other on sight," Cole told her sardonically.

Kelsey snapped her head around, outraged. "Damn it, I do not intend to sit here while you two crack little inside jokes. Tell me why those two men didn't attack us!"

"Probably because they couldn't figure out what Cole was doing with you. He's the wild card in all this," Valentine explained.

"Now tell me what happens next. You both seem to have devised all sorts of clever schemes in the space of a few short minutes. In fact, everyone around here except me seems to have some idea of what's going on. I can think of a couple of reasons why that state of affairs exists!"

"What reasons, Kelsey?" Valentine asked, sounding genuinely curious.

"The first possibility, of course, is the fact that you're both just a hell of a lot smarter than I am," she remarked scathingly.

"And the second?" Cole inquired too softly.

"The second is that everyone already knows what's going to happen next because the whole thing's been planned from the start. I'm just playing the role of pawn."

Utter silence greeted that comment. Kelsey shivered, and it wasn't from the creepiness of the cave. The tremor went through her because she had just now realized the truth of her words. She was sitting meekly between two men who seemed to be taking a dangerous situation with a frightening degree of calm. That calm could easily stem from the fact that they both knew exactly what was going on.

It was Cole who broke the tense silence. He looked across at Valentine and his mouth curved wryly. "I believe I mentioned earlier that Kelsey doesn't quite understand she's not an independent anymore."

"Not an independent what?" she demanded fiercely.

"He only means that you belong to him, Kelsey." Valentine spoke soothingly. "It's all right. You've had a rough day and this is all very confusing. You just sit tight here in this cave while Stockton and I go have a look around. We won't be gone long."

"But how will you know where to look? Cibola may not be very large as islands go, but there's still a great deal of terrain out there where someone could be hiding. Especially at night."

"Well, I've been keeping tabs on the situation since dawn." Valentine smiled gently. "I have a pretty good idea of where to look for our two visitors. They were watching the landing strip when Ray dropped you off. They started to follow you back to my place to see what you'd do. Stockton lost them when he dragged you back down the hill taking the scenic route. Our two friends are sticking to the few footpaths we have around here. They don't seem very comfortable in the wilds. In fact, I get the feeling they've spent most of their lives on city streets."

"So where will they be now?" Kelsey asked.

"Where would you spend the night around here if you had a choice?" Valentine asked blandly.

"If I had a choice? Your nice, comfortable house, complete with food and power!" Kelsey answered unhesitatingly.

"And that's probably exactly what our friends will do." Cole got to his feet and walked to the cave entrance. "It will be completely dark in another half hour. They won't want to be caught out in the open. They also know we aren't likely to try hiking over those hills to the village. Not at night."

"They've probably got someone keeping an eye on things in the village, anyway, just on the off chance that we did make a try for it. Possibly the guy who piloted the launch away from the bay this morning," Valentine added consideringly. "The town is very tiny. It would be easy to watch the harbor entrance to make certain no one left aboard a boat."

"So we assume they'll spend the night on guard at your place, planning to resume the search for us at dawn. That gives us most of the night. The launch will probably return in the morning."

"No sooner than that," Valentine agreed, rising to his full height. "This whole side of the island is protected by some rough reefs. That little bay you saw is one of the few points a boat can be brought close to shore, and even it would be too tricky to try at night. You have to be able to see what you're doing out there."

"I wonder why those two thugs didn't arrange to have the launch return and take them off the island before nightfall," Kelsey mused aloud.

"I imagine they've been paid very well to get those

printouts, Kelsey," Valentine said. "If they leave the island they run the risk of losing track of us completely."

"What I don't quite understand," Kelsey went on very carefully, "is just what you two are planning to do. What can you hope to accomplish running around out there in the dark? If you think you know where those creeps are spending the night, why go observe? Let's just all stay hidden here until dawn and then hike on over to the village to call for help."

Both Cole and Valentine turned to stare at her as if she'd just said something outrageous instead of highly practical.

"Honey, you don't understand," Cole finally said. "Tonight is simply too good an opportunity to miss. Those two are all alone up there in Valentine's house. If we move tonight, we can take them out."

"Take them out where?" Kelsey asked blankly, and then realization dawned. "Take them! You're going to go up there and try to capture them?" Horrified, she jumped to her feet. "I forbid it! As the highest ranking representative of the Flex-Glad Corporation present, I absolutely refuse to sanction such an action."

"Kelsey," Cole began carefully while Valentine turned politely away to study the landscape. "You may be the highest ranking Flex-Glad employee present since you're the *only* employee here, but—"

"Don't forget Valentine," she snapped.

"He isn't exactly an employee, is he?"

"More like an independent contractor," Valentine put in soothingly. "I don't take orders from anyone. Not any more."

Kelsey was incensed. "I do not intend to split hairs.

On behalf of Flex-Glad, I am refusing to let you carry out such a ridiculously dangerous project." She stood with her hands planted on the hips of her stained jeans, her hazel eyes almost green as they flashed her anger and frustration.

Cole stepped forward, capturing her face between rough palms. His gaze burned down into hers. "Kelsey, honey, this is the way it has to be."

"According to you!"

He nodded once. "According to me. I know what I'm doing. You're going to have to trust me."

"You keep saying that," she wailed helplessly, knowing already that she didn't stand a chance of stopping him.

"I suppose I keep saying it because I keep hoping that you will."

She brushed that aside. "This isn't a matter of trust. It's a question of logical behavior under difficult circumstances. You and Valentine are not behaving in a practical, logical fashion!"

A strange little smile played briefly around Cole's mouth. "Don't expect logic from an ex-ballet dancer. I go for style."

"Damn it, Cole, this is not a joke!" She could feel the tears burning at the back of her eyes and only an effort of will kept them from falling. "My God, why am I even trying to reason with you? I have absolutely no influence at all over you, do I?"

"How can I help but be influenced by you, Kelsey?" he asked her grittily. "You're the reason we're here!"

She stared at him. "Then listen to me. Don't go chasing off into the jungle tonight. Stay here and in the morning we'll find a way over to the village to get help."

Valentine interrupted in a husky growl. "Kelsey, there isn't any help to be had in the village. There are only a few fishing families there, none of whom will want to get involved in this fracas. By the time I can summon help from one of the larger islands, those two at the house will be gone."

"Let them disappear!"

Cole dropped his hands from her face, his expression remote and hard. "No, Kelsey. We can't do that."

He seemed to lose interest in making her understand and Kelsey was stricken numb by a tangle of emotions that contained everything from fury to despair. Wordlessly she sank back down on the rock she had been using for a stool, her arms wrapped tightly around her as she stared sightlessly out into the darkness.

Time passed. She was aware of Cole and Valentine deciding to wait for the rise of the moon so they could use its light to make their way up to the octagonal house. She heard Valentine speaking quietly of something he had taken out of the house that morning and left stashed near it. She knew that Cole tried more than once to discern her expression, but the shadows concealed her features well. Time passed, during which she said nothing, continuing to sit perfectly still in the darkness. Kelsey paid no attention to the low discussion going on between Cole and Valentine. For some strange reason everything seemed remote and unreal now.

Finally Cole reached out to put a hand on her shoulder. "It's time for us to go, Kelsey."

She didn't move. "Have fun," she said bitterly.

Valentine's huge bulk shifted in the darkness. "Kelsey, if something happens..."

She stiffened under Cole's touch but refused to acknowledge the implications of Valentine's words. Cole finished the sentence.

"Kelsey, if we don't come back in a few hours, you're to stay here in the cave until you hear or see that launch arrive and take our visitors off the island, understand? You'll be able to see the bay without being seen if you crawl outside and use the natural cover. When they've gone, start walking and don't stop until you reach the other side of the island. It will take you several hours to get there. Go down to the village and hire one of the fishermen to take you back to St. Thomas."

She ignored that, making one last plea. "Cole, please don't go."

"I'll be back as soon as I can, Kelsey." His fingers tightened on her shoulder for an instant, and then he and Valentine were gone. They both seemed to vanish into the darkness the moment they left the cave.

Kelsey put her head down onto her folded arms and let the tears flow.

A lot of thoughts went through her head during the endless time that followed. Logic insisted she recognize the fact that she really had no proof the mysterious thugs from the launch even existed. She had seen only Valentine and Cole on this island. The whole situation could be an involved plot to take the printouts without throwing any blame on either of the two men. But even as she reminded herself of that possibility,

Kelsey couldn't bring herself to really believe it. Perhaps, she decided bluntly, she just didn't want to believe it. She could take just about anything from Cole except that. It was unbearable to think that he might have lied to her from the beginning.

No. Cole didn't lie to her. He just wouldn't give her all the answers.

One thing was certain: Valentine had certainly done something more in his past than play with computers. Just as Cole had done something other than play with his business investments.

Two of a kind. Men who walked like large hunting cats through the jungle. Men who seemed familiar with the prospect of violence. She had always known there was another, darker side to Cole, but Kelsey was aware she hadn't really believed her own wild guesses about him being a part-time hit man or a loan shark.

Now she shuddered in the darkness as she contemplated just what kind of background would give Cole grim confidence in his own ability to handle the dangerous situation on the island.

It was after she had considered all those possibilities that Kelsey finally remembered something else about Cole Stockton.

Until tonight he had waged a successful campaign to keep his past locked behind closed doors. It was because of her that he was opening those gates. If she had never brought him to this island, he would not have been forced to use the dangerous skills he had learned in his other life.

The sudden pain that coursed through her at the thought of having caused Cole to unlock a past he obviously wanted to escape told Kelsey all she needed to know.

She had fallen in love with him.

The remote-control computer keyboard was lying undisturbed exactly where Valentine had left it. He pushed aside a pile of palm fronds and picked it up.

Cole grinned savagely in the moonlight as he glanced at the keyboard and then at Valentine's satisfied expression. They were several yards from the house, which was ablaze with lights. There was no doubt the unwelcome tourists were inside.

"The computer controls just about everything in the house, including a few special touches I've installed over the past couple of years," Valentine murmured.

"And you control the computer with that keyboard." Cole nodded. "Kelsey has told me about the remote controls on some of the new home computers. The keyboards don't have to be connected physically to the machines. How does it work?"

"Infrared signals. I've beefed this sucker up quite a bit. It will function at a distance of up to a hundred feet." Valentine patted the object in his hand with paternal pride.

"So we use it to douse the lights. That should give our friends a start," Cole remarked.

"And then I'll key the storm shutters to lock in place. That will seal up the windows. No one ever understood why I wanted locking metal shutters on all my windows," he said dryly.

"No one ever understood why I doubled the height of my garden walls when I bought my home in Carmel.

I think Kelsey was scared to death to go inside for fear she'd never get out again. She calls it a fortress."

"It's hard to explain to a woman how one picks up such extreme security habits," Valentine wryly pointed out.

"Yeah. Something tells me she didn't buy the dance-school bit," Cole muttered sardonically.

"What have you been telling her up to this point?"

Cole sighed. "Nothing. Nothing at all."

"And you expect that to work?"

"It hasn't been what you'd call incredibly successful. She's as curious as a cat."

"And you've been stonewalling."

"I figured she'd hate the truth far more than she'd hate the silence," Cole said with a shrug.

"Hard to say. Women are funny creatures." Valentine was quiet for a moment, his thumb idly stroking the keyboard in his big hands. He studied Cole's face in the moonlight. "Start out in the military?" he asked finally.

Cole nodded. "You?"

"Southeast Asia. I was very young. It all seemed like an adventure back then. When the sense of adventure wore off it just seemed unreal."

"I know. And then one day you realize it's become a business. At least it did for me. You wonder what the hell you've turned into." Cole glanced toward the house.

"You went free-lance?"

"When I got out of the army I had no reason to go back to the States. I stayed in Southeast Asia. There were plenty of jobs for men who knew their way around that part of the world and who weren't too fussy about how they earned their pay. Some of the most lucrative were those Uncle Sam was offering," Cole added.

"High paying, short-term contracts. No questions asked, no help from the government if you screw up."

"But lots of cash quietly deposited in a numbered account in Switzerland. I took the jobs. There didn't seem any reason not to."

"I know that feeling of not having any reason not to take the contracts." Valentine was silent for a moment as they both let the truth lie unvarnished between them. "The trick in life seems to be making your own reasons for doing things. I went the mercenary route for a few years. Africa and South America mostly, fighting other people's wars. And then I discovered I have this...empathy with computers. Long story."

"With an ending here on Cibola, hmm?"

Valentine nodded seriously, shaking off the past. "This is home. And right now two uninvited guests are intruding."

"I know how I'd feel if I found someone had got past my garden walls without an invitation," Cole said evenly. "What else can that gadget do besides seal the windows and douse the lights?"

"It can trigger the valve on a canister of gas I keep tucked into the ceiling. Very unpleasant gas. As soon as it's released we're going to have two very miserable men lurching through the front door, gasping for air."

"Then we'd better have the welcome mat out." Cole reached for the palm fronds that had been shielding the computer keyboard and began to bind them together. He worked until he had a long, tough rope of vegetation. When he was finished he glanced up at Valentine. "Ready when you are, maestro."

They moved together toward the edge of the clearing. Every room in the octagonal house was lit, but whoever was inside was prudently steering clear of the windows.

"They probably know we're unarmed," Valentine mused. "Ray would have told them you weren't carrying anything lethal, and when they went through my place at dawn they were bound to see I had no ammunition stores. I'm sure they feel very safe in there. The bastards."

Cole understood the sentiments. "Hit the lights," he ordered softly.

Valentine depressed three keys on the board and instantly the house went dark. Cole didn't wait to see if there was any reaction from within. He moved out into the open, crossing the clearing as rapidly as possible. It would take a while for the two inside to decide what was going on, and he had to take advantage of those few seconds of disorientation. They'd assume something had gone wrong with the generator.

He went down on his belly in front of the door, slinging the crude rope around the post that held the awning. Letting it lie loose on the ground, he waited for Valentine to trigger the next sequence of events.

There were sounds coming from inside the house now. Hoarsely muttered commands and angry oaths. A second later there was a grating, metallic rush of noise as Valentine ordered the computer to seal the windows. Now there was only one exit: the front door.

Someone inside panicked. A shot roared through the night, and the bullet pierced the door panel over Cole's head. He hugged the ground and waited for the next step.

Cole never heard the hiss the escaping gas made, but he was well aware of the reaction of the men inside the house. Screams of panic gave way to retching, gasping sounds. Two more shots slammed through the door, and then it was shoved open. Firing wildly, two men floundered over the threshold.

Cole used the palm-frond rope to trip the first yelling man. Already reeling, the guy hit the dirt with a thud, allowing time for Cole to deal with the second intruder.

Coming to his feet in a smooth arc of energy, Cole brought the side of his fist down on the second man's neck. He fell as if he'd been pole-axed.

A wave of the noxious gas caught Cole as it seeped through the doorway. He backed off hurriedly, frantically inhaling fresh air. The first man was struggling to his knees as Cole swung around. It was almost an unconscious reaction to put the guy out with a blow from the heel of his hand.

Cole left both men where they lay and raced out of reach of the dissipating gas. "Hell, Valentine, that stuff is god-awful!"

"I'm glad you approve," Valentine drawled as he came forward. "A little something I picked up while working for a very technologically oriented sheikh. I keep a gas mask in the drawer beside my bed. Always thought I'd probably be in the house myself, if I ever had to use it."

"Well, it's a cinch no one's going to be able to spend the night in there," Cole growled as he helped Valentine secure the two men on the ground.

"I suggest you leave these two with me. They don't look like they're going to give anyone any trouble. I've spent many a night out in the open. We'll ask them a few pertinent questions before you leave, and then you can go spend the night in that cave. I've got some food I can send with you. Your lady will be waiting."

Cole glanced up as he finished binding the feet of the second unconscious intruder. "Waiting to do what?" he wondered aloud. "Scream at me? Accuse me of plotting this whole mess? Demand that I never come near her again?"

Valentine tilted his head in the moonlight, his rather savage grin gleaming through his beard. "You won't know what kind of a welcome you'll get until you go down to the cave and find out, will you?"

EIGHT

He had known nights such as this one before now. They always ended in a strange tangle of emotions that were better buried than examined.

Cole made his way down the path toward the sea, veering off in the direction of the cave as he came out onto the beach. He didn't need the flashlight Valentine had provided. The huge tropical moon bathed the landscape in a pale glow that could have been romantic to another man. Cole had never thought of moonlight in such a way. It was usually a factor to be cursed because it illuminated too well. Yet occasionally he had been very grateful for the light.

It had been a while since he had used the gleam of such a moon to find his way home after an evening of violence—no, "home" was the wrong word. He had never used the moonlight for that purpose because he had never had a home to which he could return afterward. He had simply used it to walk away from one job to a place that served as a resting point before going on to another.

Home had never been waiting at the end of the

moon's path, and neither had a particular woman. Tonight there would be a cave and Kelsey. Tonight seemed very different from all the other nights.

The violence this evening had been minimal. He had known far worse. Strange that the aftermath was as fierce as it had ever been. The adrenaline was still throbbing in his bloodstream and the primitive but controlled sensation of savagery still simmered along with it. Both would fade. He knew that much from long experience. What usually followed was a restless depression. It was that which he had come to dread.

But tonight there was a new element mixed in with all the others. Tonight he was walking out of the jungle to find his woman, and he realized that what he was feeling on top of everything else was a heightened sense of anticipation and anxiety.

The two emotions flared through him, tangling and writhing until he felt as though they were pulling him apart.

Brutally he tried first to crush the anticipation. There was no reason to think Kelsey would throw herself into his arms. It was sheer fantasy to imagine such a scene. She had been sitting huddled into herself when he had left, completely withdrawn. Her despair and anger had been palpable in the confines of the cave. The most he could expect from her was a polite, remote concern. She would want to know what had happened. Probably ask after Valentine. Then she'd ask about the two in the cabin.

Questions. That's what he could expect tonight. A hundred cool questions. And she had a right to hear the answers this time. She had been a part of it. When he had given her all the explanations she would probably turn her back on him and try to get some rest. It was unreasonable to think she would forgive him for not trying to do things her way. Kelsey would not understand the need for the violence.

It was also unreasonable for him to expect complete trust tonight. She had every right to question his role in this mess. Every right to wonder if she wasn't a pawn in some elaborate scheme concocted by him.

In time that end of things could be straightened out, but it wasn't likely to happen tonight. He had no proof to offer that he had acted only to defend and protect her.

If he was totally honest with himself he had to admit that in her place he probably would be formulating conspiracy theories, too. No, not *probably*, definitely. After all, he was accustomed to thinking in terms of betrayal and violence. It would be natural for him to question the role of those around him. Kelsey was an intelligent woman. He could expect cautious, intelligent questions and a prudent degree of distrust when he gave her the answers.

After that lecture to himself, it wasn't too hard to suppress the sense of anticipation that had been welling up in him. The anxiety replaced it easily.

Cole's night vision was good. With the aid of the moon it was no major task to work his way through the tumbled rocks that littered the bluff above the beach. With an unerring sense of direction that he long ago had learned to take for granted, he headed for the tangled undergrowth that shielded the cave entrance.

The adrenaline had dissipated, but the tension remained. He was strangely weary, but he knew already he wouldn't be able to sleep for a long while yet. Cole could read his immediate future as if it were written in stone. He could expect to lie awake for hours tonight, aware of Kelsey beside him, holding herself physically and emotionally apart. The image caused a grim despair to course through him.

Kelsey never heard his approach, but she was aware of his presence the moment he appeared in the wide mouth of the cave.

She leaped to her feet, staring hungrily at the dark shape of him. Desperately she tried to read his face in the dim glow of the moon. All she could see was the familiar, hard planes of his jaw and the stern line of his mouth. The gray eyes were far too shadowed. There was no way she could discern the emotions in them.

"Cole! Oh, my God, Cole! I've been so worried." She waited in absolute stillness, and then the paralysis broke. Kelsey hurled herself forward, straight into his arms and buried her face against his shoulder.

He was safe. Nothing else mattered just then. The knowledge sang through her, pushing aside all the doubts and agonizing fears of the past few hours.

"Kelsey?"

There was an odd note of disbelief in his voice. Perhaps it was confusion. She ignored it, wrapping her arms fiercely around his lean waist and clinging as though her life depended on it.

"You're all right? You aren't hurt?" she demanded huskily.

His hands moved slowly, almost tentatively on her back and then circled her with sudden power. Cole lowered his head, seeking the shell of her ear. "I'm okay. I'm fine. Kelsey, I..."

"And Valentine? Is he okay?"

"Yes. Everything went like clockwork. Valentine's staying at the cabin tonight to keep an eye on the two we caught. We're going to have to sleep here, I'm afraid. Valentine's house isn't habitable at the moment." He broke off as if searching for other words. "Kelsey, I'm sorry about tonight. I didn't have any choice. Please believe me, if there had been any other way—"

"Hush," she whispered, aware of the strange tension in him and wanting nothing more than to soothe. Her fingers trailed tenderly along the muscles of his neck, massaging the skin beneath the collar of his khaki shirt. "Hush, darling. You need to rest. There's no reason to talk just now. Is there anything else you have to do tonight? Is it all over?"

"It's over for tonight," he said, sighing. "In the morning we'll have to pick up the third man. The two we caught at the cabin said he was due right after dawn. But for tonight it's over. Kelsey, I know this has been hard for you."

"All I had to do was sit in the dark with a bunch of lizards. You were the one who had to go out and exert yourself." She smiled tremulously, slipping free of his arms to take his hand. "I disobeyed orders a couple of times, though." She started leading him to the far side of the cave.

"What are you talking about?" Sudden disapproval flashed into his voice and he halted at once. "Kelsey, what have you done?"

"A relatively small act of insubordination. I just ducked outside earlier and gathered some ferns to spread on the ground. There was a lot of greenery growing very thickly near the cave entrance. Since we're going to have to spend the night here, it's lucky I found something to cushion these rocks, isn't it?"

He continued to stand, unmoving. "You shouldn't have left the cave without permission. Kelsey, I told you to stay put."

She came back into his arms. He sounded so weary, yet so determined to stay in command of the situation. What he needed was rest and time to recover from whatever had happened up at the cabin. With feminine intuition guiding her, Kelsey nestled against him. "I'm sorry, Cole. It won't happen again."

"Oh, hell, what am I doing," he muttered, letting her push him down onto the bed of ferns she had contrived earlier. "There was no harm done, and the last thing I want to do tonight is yell at you."

"You rarely yell," she assured him gently. "Are you certain you're all right?" She came down on her knees beside him. "What have you got there?" she asked, glancing at a packet he was carrying.

"You rarely yell," she assured him gently. "Are you certain you're all right?" She came down on her knees beside him. "What have you got there?" she asked, glancing at a packet he was carrying.

"Valentine sent some cheese and bread."

"Thank goodness. I'm starving."

They munched the food in silence. When it was finished, Kelsey leaned toward Cole.

"What are you doing, Kelsey?" He stared down at

her hands as they moved in the moonlight. She was unbuttoning his shirt.

"You're as tense as a coiled spring. I'm going to rub your back for you. Otherwise you aren't going to sleep a wink tonight."

His head lifted abruptly. "You want to rub my back?" He sounded disoriented.

"That's right. Turn over and use your arms for a pillow. My God. Every muscle is like a sheet of steel," she muttered as he slowly did as she directed.

"I must smell like a herd of buffalo," he growled.

"Not quite. But then I'm not exactly a rose garden myself at the moment. It's been a long day."

"You always smell good," he said with great certainty. "I used to think about your special scent at odd times during the week when you were in San Jose."

"Did you?" she asked shyly. Her hands worked on his broad back and she took satisfaction in the slow relaxation of his body.

"Yes." He paused as if gathering his thoughts. "Kelsey, I know you must have a lot of questions," he finally began hesitantly.

"You can tell me all the details in the morning. Right now you need to stop thinking and just relax. You need sleep."

"I need you," he said with sudden harshness. "I've never needed you more than I do tonight."

Kelsey heard the raw hunger in him and her hands stilled. "I'm here, Cole."

He turned over slowly on his back, seeking her face in the moonlight. "Just like that?"

She sucked in her breath, her love for him sweeping

aside everything else. "Just like that," she agreed gently. She leaned over and feathered his lips with her own, longing to give him whatever he wanted from her.

"Oh, Kelsey!" Cole put his arms around her with a strength that told its own story. He pulled her down on top of his bare chest, his legs snarling with hers.

The strong male scent of his body filled Kelsey's nostrils and the power in his grasp conveyed an urgency she had no wish to deny. She did not fully understand this man; knew that she would never be privy to his secrets; recognized that he wasn't the tender, communicative lover she had always wanted for herself. But this was the man with whom she had fallen in love.

Tonight he had gone to battle on her behalf, dealing with a dangerous situation in the only way he knew. Now he was back, needing her.

She felt his fingers move roughly down the row of buttons of her stained yellow shirt, impatiently yanking the fabric free until the once-stylish garment hung open. Cole slipped his hands inside the shirt, exhaling deeply as he grazed his palms across the tips of her breast.

"Kelsey, honey, I didn't dare let myself believe it would be like this tonight. You don't know how badly I want you. There have been women, but there's never been a particular woman waiting. Oh, hell, I can't explain it."

"Don't try." She drew her fingertips lightly over his shoulders, kissing him softly at the curve of his throat. He shuddered beneath her and gave up trying to talk.

Kelsey felt the snap of her jeans being undone, and

then he was sliding his hands inside the white denim and pushing the fabric down over her hips. Her panties went the way of the jeans, and when she lay naked along his half-clothed length Cole touched her demandingly, as if he couldn't get enough of her.

She trembled under the intensity of his caresses. When he probed between her thighs she gasped. His fingers moved gently, stroking until the dampening warmth he elicited told him of her arousal.

"I promised myself after last time that I would take all the time in the world when I finally got you back in my arms. But I didn't know it would happen like this," he said huskily. "I didn't think it would be on a hard floor of a cave, and I couldn't know it would be after I'd spent the evening trying to straighten out the mess you'd got yourself into. Kelsey, honey, why is it I never seem to be in complete control on the rare occasions I make love to you?" he concluded hoarsely.

"You've always told me I'm the one who asked too many questions." She moved a little so that she could reach the buckle of his belt.

"Are you telling me to shut up?"

She heard the rueful humor in him and put her mouth to his. "Yes," she muttered against his lips.

He took her command literally. Without a word he set her aside, sitting up so that he could yank off his boots and khaki slacks. Then he lay down beside her, cushioning himself on the ferns and moss she had gathered. Wrapping his strong hands around her waist, Cole pulled Kelsey astride his lean hips. Kelsey was abruptly, vividly aware of his heavy arousal.

"Cole?"

"No more words. Not now," he reminded her thickly. He fitted himself to her softness and held her steady while he surged upward. In one powerful thrust he invaded her clinging warmth, and her soft cry was lost beneath his groan of need.

Although Kelsey was on top, it was Cole who set the rhythm of their passion. Anchoring her at the waist, he moved within her, filling her totally and then withdrawing over and over again until Kelsey was a shivering creature of pulsating desire.

"Yes, Cole, oh, yes, *please*," she begged. Her nails scored the skin of his shoulders, and she nipped a little savagely at his hard flesh.

"Sweet she-devil," he rasped as he felt the touch of her small teeth. "There are times when you are not as civilized as you'd like to pretend!"

She couldn't answer him. His driving passion was swamping her senses, leaving her unable to think. She could only feel now; knew only the sense of being filled with his manhood; was aware only of the power in him as he held her in place for his thrusting body.

The shimmering convulsions swept up out of nowhere and shook her. She gasped brokenly, her whole body tightening.

"Kelsey!"

Cole was sucked over the edge into the vortex of the climax, his body following hers as men have always followed women. He grated her name again and again as the release pounded through him. The rough cries filled the cave and then slowly, slowly disintegrated until there was nothing left but profound and complete silence.

It was a long time before Kelsey stirred along the length of Cole's sprawled form. When she finally did he opened his eyes lazily. "Going somewhere?"

"Your backside must be a bit raw by now," she murmured, sliding down to lie alongside him. "These ferns I picked don't exactly constitute a mattress."

He allowed her to readjust her position but kept her snug against his body. Reaching for their discarded clothing, Cole spread it out beneath them, padding the mossy floor of the cave as well as he could. Then he lay back, his fingers sliding along her arm with absent pleasure.

"Thank you, Kelsey. I haven't felt this good since the last time I had you in my bed."

"This isn't your bed," she reminded him lightly. It was satisfying to feel his relaxed state and know she had been the cause of it.

"Details," he assured her dismissingly. "Wherever you are, when you're lying with me, I'm in my bed. It was just like coming home tonight when I walked into the cave and you ran into my arms. I tried to tell you there's never been a woman waiting for me," he said simply.

"Go to sleep, Cole. You must be exhausted."

"You must have a million questions," he said hesitantly, the sleepiness clear in his voice. He stifled a yawn with the back of his hand.

Kelsey took a breath. Her decision had been made during that long wait alone in the cave. "No, Cole. No questions. At least not about the past."

She felt him grow unnaturally still beside her. "What are you trying to say, Kelsey?"

"Only that I've decided to do things your way. Keep your secrets, Cole. You have a right to them. I had no business trying to pry them out of you. I trust you."

His hand tightened around her shoulders. "You do?"

"I wouldn't have stayed here waiting for you in this horrid cave if I didn't trust you," she said gently. "I won't push you ever again."

"Kelsey, honey, don't make rash promises." He sounded distinctly skeptical.

"It's not a rash promise. I had plenty of time to think about it while you were gone tonight. You're entitled to draw the lines in your life and I have no right to cross them." She touched the edge of his mouth with the tip of her finger. "I won't ask any more questions about your past. For you and I there will be only the present. I promise."

He caught her fingers and crushed them tightly in one large hand. "Kelsey, you won't regret it, I swear. I'll give you anything I can."

"I don't need anything, Cole. Only you."

"All I needed was to know you trusted me. Believe me, the past doesn't matter. The present is the only thing that counts between us."

"Yes," she whispered. "Only the present."

No past, Kelsey thought silently as she cradled her head on Cole's shoulder. *And no future. Only the present.* She would take life on a day-to-day basis. No more trying to build a future based on understanding and acceptance and communication. Cole could not offer that. She would take what she could get for as long as it lasted.

No past and no future. Only the present.

The promise had been made to herself during the interminable wait in the cave. It didn't mean the questions would go away. They still hovered in the wings. She would always wonder what kind of past Cole had that had taught him to take violence in stride. She would be curious about the likeness between Valentine and him. She was certain they had never met before yesterday, but Kelsey was equally sure they had recognized some quality in each other on sight. Even she had noted the disturbing similarities in the way they chose to deal with the dangerous situation they had encountered.

Every time she thought of her stepfather she would find herself thinking of the Stockton file locked in the computer. The question of those thousand-dollar-a-month payments to Cole was another issue that would not simply fade away, now that she had made her decision.

And every time she spent the night with Cole in his walled home she would ask herself why any man would build such a fortress in which to live.

No, the questions would never cease. Her curiosity about the man she loved would last as long as the relationship. Longer, she forced herself to acknowledge. She could not allow herself the luxury of thinking of a future. Cole lived only for the present, and if she would spend that present with him then she must learn to think in those terms, too.

The questions would continue in her mind, but Kelsey vowed they would not be asked aloud. She would

rely on the basic, underlying trust she had finally acknowledged during the long wait in the cave.

With that promise floating in her mind, Kelsey
closed her eyes and crowded deeper into Cole's protective embrace. He was sleeping, his lean hard body relaxed at last. But she felt his arm tighten instinctively
around her. A few moments later, in spite of the uncomfortable bed provided by the cave, Kelsey fell
asleep.

She awoke hours later to the very faintest rays of an
island dawn seeping through the vegetation that
guarded the cave. Then came the realization that Cole
was gone. Her next awareness was of the stiffness in
her muscles.

"Oh Lord. I may never recover from this cave," she
groaned, sitting up slowly and glancing around.
"Cole?" she called tentatively, thinking he must have
stepped outside.

An intelligent-looking lizard, brilliantly illustrated
in shades of green and blue, blinked at her from a
nearby rock.

"Voyeur," Kelsey accused, reaching for her crushed
and stained clothing. The lizard watched her dress,
clearly fascinated, and then it skittered off on more important business.

Cole had not returned by the time Kelsey had finished pulling on the garments. She stretched, trying to
limber up the muscles that had been cramped and
bruised by the hard bed, and then she went to the cave
entrance.

"Cole?" she called again, frowning into the pearling
morning light.

Still no answer. She pushed her way through the vegetation that protected the entrance and stood looking down at the sandy beach far below. Maybe Cole had decided to take a swim as a substitute for a bath. She could use one herself.

Her gaze swept across the jagged, rock-strewn slope that formed the bluff above the beach. Still no sign of Cole.

A trickle of nervousness assailed her. Damn the man. Trust was all very well and good, but this habit of disappearing in the mornings was getting to be more than a shade annoying. He had disappeared that first morning after he had made love to her, the morning after her had nursed her through the sea-sickness and now this morning. Kelsey decided her resolution not to question his past did not apply to details of his present actions.

If she was going to be forced to learn the ultimate meaning of compromise, Cole could darn well learn something about that fine art himself. Irritably Kelsey started away from the cave, moving along the rocky bluff in the general direction of the cliff that ringed the bay. She would find the path that led to Valentine's house and see if the big man knew what Cole was up to this morning.

It wasn't until she came in sight of the bay and saw the small launch anchored in it that Kelsey suddenly remembered the unfinished business Cole had alluded to last night.

A wave of panic sent her flat on her stomach. The boat carrying the third man Valentine had mentioned was down there, and a figure stood in the bow. She inched her way to the edge of the cliff and looked out. The man in the boat was armed. He was holding a high-powered rifle on Cole, who stood on the sandy beach.

Kelsey thought her breathing had stopped. A terrifying sense of helplessness seized her. She was too far away to do anything. Cole had seemed so much in command of the situation yesterday, and she knew he and Valentine had been expecting the third man's arrival. How on earth had he managed to get himself trapped down there on the beach?

Then she realized the attaché case was sitting on the sand in front of him. Cole stood easily, his booted feet planted slightly apart, his stance seemingly relaxed.

There was an air of balance in the way he stood watching the man with the rifle. Kelsey moved uncertainly, straining to see exactly what was happening. All the natural fighting balance in the world wasn't going to do much good against a man with a rifle.

Kelsey glanced around, frantically trying to find any sign of Valentine. Surely he would have accompanied Cole to this dawn rendezvous. The two men had worked together last night. She couldn't believe they hadn't planned this morning's events as a team.

The fact that Valentine was nowhere in evidence could be cause for further panic on her part, Kelsey thought morosely. Or it could mean the huge man was hidden somewhere behind a boulder on top of the cliff. Perhaps he was providing cover for Cole's actions from behind one of the tumbled piles of rocks at the bottom of the cliff.

There was no way of knowing what was really happening, she realized as panic and fury mingled in her. Neither of the two men had thought fit to inform her about what was planned for this morning. She was left to stare in horror as the man she loved stood unarmed in front of a thug with a rifle.

"Make up your mind," Cole called roughly to the man in the gently rocking boat. "It's a fair price considering what I'm offering in exchange."

"How do I know you've got the genuine article for sale?" the rifleman called back.

"You don't. Not until you come ashore and have a look at the samples I've got in the case," Cole told him laconically.

"Seems like it would be easier to kill you and then come ashore," the other man drawled consideringly.

"Easier, except you wouldn't have a snowball's chance in hell of figuring out where to start looking for those documents. They could be hidden anywhere on this island. No, I think killing me would be very risky under the circumstances. I suggest we do business together, instead."

"What about Keller and Matson?"

"Your friends are out of the picture, I'm afraid. Simple all the way around, though, isn't it? This way you get to keep whatever you make from handing over the printouts to whoever hired you. No splits."

"Except what I have to pay you," the man in the boat reminded him coldly.

"All I'm asking is fifty thousand. That seems reasonable, given the value of those papers."

"I don't have any fifty G's with me."

"So I'm prepared to wait while you go arrange things. I'll still be here when you get back."

"What about the crazy hacker who was supposed to be somewhere on the island?"

"Like your pals, he's no longer involved," Cole said succinctly.

"And the woman."

"I'll handle the woman."

Kelsey grimaced at the cold-blooded way Cole said those last words. He could sound incredibly ruthless, she thought uneasily. Perhaps because he *was* incredibly ruthless. Or had been in his past, she corrected herself. Once again she tried to scan the rock cliff top, searching for Valentine. She couldn't believe he wasn't up here somewhere, supplying cover. Cole and Valentine were two of a kind, and neither was stupid.

"I'd have to see those printouts for myself before I could agree to any deals," the man with the rifle declared.

"I'm willing to show you a couple of pages. Not the whole lot. The remainder is my insurance policy, as I'm sure you can understand." Cole indicated the attaché case with a careless glance. "If you want to come ashore and take a look, it's fine with me."

"How do I know I can trust you?"

Cole shrugged. "You don't. I brought along a sample of the product for sale. Do you want to see it or not?"

"Yeah, I'll come take a look," the other man finally decided. "Open the case and leave it on the sand. You stand over there." He waved the rifle to a point about twenty feet from the case.

Cole obediently moved away as the rifleman

stepped over the side of his boat into knee-deep water and started wading to shore.

Kelsey's fingers clenched fearfully into a small fist. Where was Valentine, she asked herself once again. She flicked a hopeless glance around the cliff, and just then light from the rising sun glinted off something metallic.

A gun barrel, Kelsey told herself, drawing a deep breath. It must be Valentine. He wasn't more than twenty feet away from her, using the huge rocks as cover.

She glanced down at the drama on the beach. The rifleman was halfway to shore now, his weapon trained unwaveringly on Cole.

Kelsey was holding her breath, wondering how and when Valentine would act when the brightening sunlight caught and held something more than the wicked sheen of metal. It illuminated the gloved hand holding the rifle. And the hand inside the thin leather glove was not one of Valentine's huge fists. Even as Kelsey watched in stunned comprehension, the gleaming metal moved forward. A second later she saw the head of the man who held the weapon. He was crawling through the rocks toward the edge of the cliff.

It wasn't Valentine. This man was small and wiry and very ratlike.

The significance of what she was seeing registered immediately. Valentine might very well be covering Cole from some other point, but neither he nor Cole could be aware of this new intruder.

She could see the stranger quite clearly now as he moved from the cover of one boulder to another. He was concentrating totally on his goal and had not spotted her.

Twenty feet away, she thought shakily. *He's only twenty feet away.*

Hidden behind her own rocky protection, Kelsey tried frantically to think. The light sound of the surf was bouncing up the face of the cliff, providing some assurance that the newcomer would not hear her if she was to move. And since the gunman was focusing intently on the scene below, he might not see her if she was exceedingly careful.

There was no way of knowing exactly what Valentine and Cole had planned. She was operating completely in the dark. But surely they could not have anticipated this new element. Valentine had been telling Cole from the beginning that there were only three men involved.

The man off to her right was clearly a backup for the one in the boat. If Valentine and Cole made a move to capture the guy down on the beach, this one would probably shoot to kill.

The image of Cole lying dead in the sand forced Kelsey to act. If she was going to do something, it had to be now. Cautiously she tried to move, and for a split second Kelsey was afraid that the combination of terror and stiff muscles might make even a small movement impossible. Then the short-lived paralysis died beneath the necessity of saving Cole.

Ever so slowly, hugging the uneven surface of the top of the bluff, Kelsey slid toward the shelter of another rock. If the gunman didn't glance back she should be safe. He was at the edge of the cliff, looking down. His rifle was aimed with steady hands. She knew his whole attention was on the scene below. Kelsey made it to the cover of a second boulder.

Ten feet away, she crouched behind a rocky projection and risked a peek around the edge. The second gunman was flat on his stomach, holding the rifle.

What now, she asked herself. Hastily she examined the limited selection of weapons at hand. Rocks and pebbles of all different sizes littered the terrain. Her insides turned sickeningly at the thought of trying to use one of the jagged stones against the intruder's head.

What if she missed, she wondered frantically. On the other hand, what if she didn't miss? The image of a crushed skull was almost her undoing.

But the overpowering mental picture of Cole's blood seeping into the sand was far more persuasive. There was no time to debate the issue. The joker from the boat would be walking up the beach now toward the attaché case. At any second Valentine would probably act, popping out from some hiding point at the base of the cliff to surprise the intended victim.

And when all that action took place, it was a sure bet that the second rifleman would act. Someone was almost bound to be killed in the ensuing melee. Someone like Cole.

Kelsey's hands closed around a rock the size of her two fists. Rising to her knees, she looked over the edge of her protective boulder and caught her breath. The second gunman still lay flat, pointing the rifle downward. With all her strength, Kelsey leaped to her feet and hurled the rock straight for his balding head.

She heard the sickening thud, for which she had

tried to prepare herself as the rock struck the man, but the sound was drowned out almost immediately by the ferocious roar of the rifle. Her victim had squeezed reflexively on the trigger as the blow had landed.

Before Kelsey could race forward to see if the gunman was truly out of commission, a second shot rang out. She threw herself flat and scrambled frantically to the cliff edge. Beside her the second gunman lay awesomely still. His weapon had fallen from his hands. She was afraid to look at his head.

Down below on the beach there was a hoarse cry. By the time she looked over the edge, Cole was sweeping up the rifle the first gunman had dropped. The man from the boat was down on his knees, clutching at his shoulder. Even as she watched, Cole swung the rifle upward, aiming for the spot where she lay. Valentine was surging up from behind a clump of rocks he had been using for cover near the base of the cliff. The gun he had just used on the man from the boat was also swinging in her direction.

"Hey, guys, it's me!" Kelsey yelped, getting hastily to her feet. "Don't shoot. I'm on your side, remember?"

A mild form of hysterical relief seemed to be assailing her. It died almost instantly as she realized that both Cole and Valentine were still aiming their weapons in her direction. She suddenly understood just how dumb it had been to leap up and yell at them.

Both men were balanced on a knife-edge of violent readiness. They were reacting to the rifle shot that had come from the top of the cliff. She suddenly realized she was lucky to be alive. It would have been second nature for either of these men to shoot first and ask questions later. Kelsey froze. The fact that she was still standing on the edge of the cliff and not lying dead at the bottom was a fact that could be credited only to the lightning swift reaction times of both Cole and Valentine.

Kelsey swallowed uncomfortably as both men slowly lowered their weapons. In that moment she recognized how dangerous both Cole and Valentine really were.

"Kelsey! What the hell do you think you're doing? Get down!"

Kelsey leaned over and picked up the rifle beside her. "It's okay, Cole," she called out unsteadily. "The guy up here is out of commission."

A low oath sliced through the air, and then Cole was racing for the uneven cliff path, covering the distance to the top in only a few seconds. Behind him, Valentine examined their captive.

Kelsey turned to face Cole as he came toward her. She read the chilling expression on his face and shivered. He halted in front of her, his glance going briefly to the unconscious man at her feet and then to the rifle in her hand.

"What in blazes are you doing out here, lady? You're supposed to be back in that cave. Who gave you permission to leave it?" He snapped the weapon from her fingers and did something quickly to the mechanism. Then he tossed it down and reached for Kelsey, giving her a fierce shake. "Answer me, woman! How dare you disobey orders like this! You could have been killed."

"So could you," she managed, although her heart

was pounding as the fear-induced adrenaline shot through her. "You didn't know about this one up here, did you?"

"No, by God, I didn't. But that is absolutely no excuse for you to be running around out here in the open. Hell, Kelsey, I ought to use my belt on your sweet tail. I ought to make sure you couldn't sit down for a week! Do you have any idea just how close you came to getting yourself killed?"

From out of nowhere, Kelsey's natural assertiveness finally revived. "It's all your fault, Cole Stockton," she shot back, infuriated by his actions. "You and your little secrets. You didn't bother to tell me what was going on. You didn't see any need to explain the plans you and Valentine had developed. You didn't think it was necessary to keep me informed or to involve me in any way, did you? Your secretiveness almost got both of us killed. But don't let that small fact interfere with the way you've chosen to run your life. Go ahead and wall yourself up behind your damn secrets! There may not be much of a future in that but, then, you don't care about the future, anyway, do you?"

She whirled, intent on getting away from him before she disgraced herself with tears. She almost stumbled over the man she had struck with the rock.

First things first, Kelsey thought with a sigh as she knelt down beside the too-quiet gunman. Right now she had to face the consequences of her own act of violence. With shaking fingers she tentatively touched the back of the man's head. He was bleeding.

"He'll live," Cole said brusquely, dropping down

beside her and investigating the wound with an expert touch. "You didn't kill him, Kelsey."

She looked across at him with mute thankfulness and had the impression he understood how hard it would have been for her to accept that she might have killed someone, even a ratlike thug such as this.

NINE

They caught the cruise ship at its next port of call. Kelsey had several reservations about continuing with the trip, and she didn't hesitate to make them known. By the time Cole managed to get her back to her stateroom he was feeling a vast sense of relief. He needed the next few days alone with Kelsey. Instinct told him that while he had won a great deal during that day and night on Cibola, the groundwork of his affair with Kelsey was still vague and shaky in many areas.

Before he could risk taking her home and finding himself competing once again with the other forces in her life he needed to establish the basis of the relationship.

He had never worried very much about relationships, he'd reflected more than once during the trip on the strongly scented fishing boat. Worrying about relationships came into the same category as panic and uncertainty. A very alien thing.

"Matters such as this have to be reported to the authorities," she had exclaimed when Valentine casually announced he could arrange to have a fishing boat from the village take them to the island where the luxury liner was due next. "Cole and I can't just take off and leave you to explain everything."

"I don't see why not," Valentine had said politely.

"But the authorities will have a lot of questions when they come to pick up these four men," Kelsey had pointed out.

"Maybe. If the authorities who were going to show up were proper FBI types and if they were arriving at your doorstep in San Jose to take these four jokers into custody. But the folks who will be coming to Cibola aren't going to be representing the U.S. government. This isn't U.S. territory, remember? Cibola is part of a very loosely knit group of islands under independent rule. Frankly, our version of the 'authorities' could care less about such exotic things as industrial espionage."

"What will they do with these four?" Kelsey had glanced worriedly at the well-secured men who had been brought around the island on the launch to the small village.

"Officially, they'll probably be accused of breaking and entering," Valentine had offered slowly.

"And unofficially?" Kelsey had pressed.

"Unofficially, their biggest crime is being four off-islanders who bothered a local resident. Being an off-islander around here is bad enough. Bothering a local is just about the worst crime in the book."

"What makes you a local? Aren't you an off-islander, too?" Kelsey had demanded.

"Not anymore," Valentine had said, chuckling. "I

did a favor for the governor on the main island a few years ago. Since then I've had official 'local' status."

"What sort of favor?" Kelsey had gone on to ask.

Cole had decided he'd better step in at that point. There was no telling what sort of dirty work Valentine might once have done for the governor, and whatever it was it would probably put even more questions into Kelsey's head.

"That's enough, Kelsey. Just take Valentine's word that he can handle matters, okay? There's no need to go into detail. You've caused enough trouble for one day."

"*I've* caused enough trouble!" she'd flared. "I may have saved your lives by being up on that cliff when I was!"

"She's right, you know," Valentine had put in mildly, obviously amused by Cole's heavy-handed approach to dealing with Kelsey.

Cole had shot him a sardonic glance. "I know, but I don't think she realizes how close she came to getting herself killed."

"Believe me, I'm well aware of it!" Kelsey had muttered.

Cole knew she was remembering the precarious seconds she had stood on the top of the cliff, facing the weapons he and Valentine had instinctively aimed in her direction. He suppressed a grim shudder. It was going to be a while before he forgot that little scene himself.

The distraction had worked. Kelsey had been successfully led away from any more questions about the favor Valentine had done for the governor. After that there had been plenty to do, what with finding an obliging fisherman, securing the four thugs in the storeroom of a local bar and saying goodbye to Valentine.

"I'll send a cable to Gladwin and let him know he's got a leak somewhere," Valentine had promised Kelsey when she expressed a few more concerns about leaving the scene of the crime. "He'll know how to handle it. These four were obviously just hired hands."

"How will Walt know where to start looking for the real source of trouble?"

"I'm sure our pals in the storeroom will be glad to give us some leads," Valentine had said easily. "I'll have a chat with them before they get taken off Cibola."

Kelsey looked dubious. "'A chat'?"

Once again Cole had deemed it prudent to step in. "Come on, Kelsey. The guy with the boat is waiting."

"But, Cole, I still think we should do something more, well, official about all this," she had protested worriedly.

"This isn't the States, Kelsey. Things work differently in other parts of the world. Valentine knows what he's doing. Let him do it," Cole had ordered firmly as he'd pulled her determinedly toward the waiting boat.

She'd turned to Valentine, who was pacing alongside her. "You're sure you'll be all right?"

"I'll be just fine, Kelsey."

"You'll come and see us if you ever get back to the States?"

"Send me an invitation to the wedding and see if I don't show up," Valentine had replied with a grin.

Cole had experienced an odd rush of annoyance when Kelsey had looked startled, and then had hastened to explain there was no wedding planned.

"Cole and I don't think too much about the future," she'd told Valentine very seriously.

Valentine had given Cole an empathic glance, and then he'd shrugged his massive shoulders. "Sometimes the future has a way of forcing itself on you. Take care, you two. I have a feeling we'll be seeing each other again sometime."

Cole had watched Kelsey brush Valentine's cheek with her soft mouth, and then he'd shaken the huge man's paw.

"If you, uh, ever need anything," Cole had begun gruffly, "yell."

"I will. And the same goes for you." Valentine had stepped back to let Kelsey climb on board the bobbing boat, and then he grinned at Cole. "Don't worry. I'll be giving Gladwin that version of the story we agreed on this morning. And about that favor I did for the governor a while back," he'd murmured for Cole's ears alone. "All I did was computerize the island's government records. The governor loves the prestige of having the most sophisticated filing system in the Caribbean. Gives him all sorts of clout when he mingles with the leaders of the other islands."

"I'll tell Kelsey," Cole had remarked wryly.

"You do that. The woman already has to deal with enough secrets. See you."

Hours later Cole dressed for dinner in his own stateroom. The shower had felt terrific, and although he wasn't wild about wearing dinner jackets and ties, the dark color of his fresh clothing was comfortable and familiar nighttime attire.

He knotted the tie with impatient efficiency and met his own brooding gaze in the mirror. He had been trying to decide on how to deal with Kelsey tonight and he still wasn't certain of the right approach.

That damned uncertainty again. Something about that woman left him feeling suspended in midair. He turned away from the mirror and reached for his jacket. One thing *was* certain. She was going to be spending the night with him. No more excuses, rationalizations, protests or other crazy, illogical feminine reasons for keeping him at arm's length.

She'd committed herself last night. Cole had no intention of allowing her to wriggle free of the implied and implicit surrender she had made there on the floor of the cave.

That knowledge brought some sense of relief, but it didn't dispel the uncertainty he was feeling. He glanced at the neatly made bunk and mentally pictured Kelsey lying in it. His body hardened at the image.

Inhaling deeply, Cole stalked toward the cabin door, wondering how it was possible to simultaneously want to take a woman to bed and yell at her. He still hadn't recovered from the close call that morning.

He strode down the corridor toward the elevator, lost in glowering thought. Kelsey had given him a great deal last night. He knew that at last she had given him her trust.

It should have been enough, he told himself as he waited for the elevator. It had certainly constituted the biggest hurdle. She had promised there would be no more questions about the past, and then she had given herself to him unreservedly.

It should have been enough. All that was left now was to work out the details of the affair. He could afford to compromise for a while, he decided as he stepped into the elevator and punched the number of Kelsey's deck. He could afford to accommodate himself to her life-style for a time.

Aware of a pleasantly magnanimous feeling, he stepped out of the elevator and headed for Kelsey's room. Now that he had the essential element of trust from her he would be generous and allow her to re-shape her life at her own pace. He was not an unreasonable man, he assured himself. He could make compromises.

Just so long as he knew that one way or another he could be certain of having Kelsey in his bed.

Kelsey moved to answer the knock on her stateroom door with a sense of determination. She had dressed for the evening knowing that in some ways she was going into the kind of negotiations that always followed a battle. Cole had won the war. Now she faced the task of working out the terms of her own surrender.

The bold, fluid shape of the chili-colored wrap dress swirled lightly around her knees. The neckline was an exciting plunge that was halted by the firm clasp of a wide, silver-studded belt. High-heeled sandals in the same shade as the dress added the height she felt she needed tonight. After spending nearly an hour in the shower washing the dirt of Cibola out of her hair, Kelsey had brushed the tawny mass until it moved around her shoulders in a smooth, well-behaved style. She was as ready as she would ever be. Kelsey opened the door.

"I think," Cole murmured thoughtfully as he stood examining the deep neckline of her dress, "that we may have to buy you a few new items for your lingerie wardrobe."

"Like what?" Kelsey hadn't been prepared for the remark.

"Like some new bras. Don't you ever wear one?"

"To work," she assured him promptly, stepping through the door to join him in the corridor. "I had no idea you were so conventional, Cole." Her mouth curved faintly.

He appeared to be waiting for a follow-up remark as he took her arm in a possessive grasp and started her toward the elevator.

"Don't hold your breath, Cole," she said gently. "I'm not going to say it."

"Say what?"

"Something about how your conventional feelings about lingerie just goes to show what little I know about you," she said readily. "You needn't worry, I'm really quite reformed. I meant it last night when I said we would ignore the past."

Beside her Cole nodded once, his expression intense. "You won't regret it, Kelsey. I've said from the beginning that the past doesn't count."

"Only the present," she agreed softly.

They dined on stuffed roulade of veal, Caesar salad and rum mousse. June and George Camden greeted Kelsey and Cole with pleasure and a great many questions about where they had spent the preceding day. Kelsey smiled serenely and let Cole handle the good-natured inquiries. He was the one who was the expert at turning aside unwanted questions, and she told him so with her bland gaze as he sat across the table from her.

"Thanks," he growled wryly as they walked out on deck after dinner. "I had no idea you could be such a reserved little creature."

"You were doing such a great job of handling all their questions I didn't want to interfere. You have a wonderful knack of being able to tell the truth without telling anyone anything," Kelsey said, laughing. "The bit about visiting an acquaintance who lives on a nearby island was masterful. At least you didn't try to give the Camdens the line about Valentine and you being ex-ballet dancers."

"You were the one who invented that one."

"So I was. Lucky for your story tonight I didn't try to give the Camdens that added tidbit." The laughter in her eyes faded as they came to a halt beside the rail.

It was a beautiful night, balmy and warm. The foaming wake of the ship was a splash of brilliant white against the darkness of the sea. Behind her the music from the cabaret sounded faintly. "Being on board ship is like being in a world apart, isn't it?" she observed after a moment. "It's as though the rest of the world with all its demands didn't exist. As though none of the problems of real life can bother you."

Cole watched her profile in the moonlight. "That's why I didn't want you to insist on going straight back to San Jose," he admitted calmly. "We need this time alone together, Kelsey. Time without any outside distractions."

She didn't pretend not to understand. "A sort of honeymoon without the wedding, hmm?"

His eyes narrowed. "You could say that. There are things we need to settle between us, honey."

"Such as?" Kelsey tried to keep her voice light and flippant. Cole's sense of humor had never been his most impressive characteristic, she reminded herself. And when he was serious, he tended to be *deadly* serious. Even Valentine, who seemed to have a lot in common with Cole, had more laughter in him than Cole would ever have.

"First of all," Cole began carefully, "I should tell you that even though I was furious with you for getting involved in that scene this morning, I was also proud of the way you handled that fourth gunman." Cole's hands flexed around the railing. "You kept your head and you pulled off a very dangerous stunt. Valentine and I may owe our lives to you. Valentine had the guy in the boat covered every second, so he was under control. But we didn't guess that a fourth man had swum ashore at another point before the boat pilot brought the launch into the bay. Since Valentine had only seen three men in the beginning, we were assuming there weren't any more. Valentine had questioned the two men we'd caught last night and they apparently didn't know about the fourth man, either, or he would have had the information out of them."

"I see. Well, it's very generous of you to thank me, Cole," Kelsey murmured dryly. "I know you've been simmering all day over that episode this morning."

"You scared the hell out of me," he told her frankly.

"I was rather scared myself." She didn't look at him, pretending to study the darkened horizon.

"Don't ever disobey me in a situation like that again, Kelsey," he ordered flatly.

"Will there be a great many more such situations, do you think?" she asked flippantly.

"I hope not. And don't make it sound as though it were all my fault," he warned. "It was your job that got you into that mess."

"And you haven't liked my job from the beginning, have you?"

"No," he said grittily. "But I am prepared to live with it for a while.

Kelsey turned her head in astonishment at the unexpected concession. "Would you mind repeating that?"

He drew a deep breath and then announced brusquely, "You heard me. I'm willing to work out a compromise regarding your job at Flex-Glad. For a while."

"What sort of compromise?" Kelsey asked cautiously.

"I'll stay with you in San Jose from Monday through Friday. I can manage an office in your apartment, I think. The weekends, holidays and vacations you will come back to my home in Carmel. Fair enough?"

"You're certainly making matters much simpler than I had expected. I was prepared for a major bit of negotiating this evening," she told him honestly. "I thought I'd have to do a great deal of talking in order to get you to agree to an arrangement like that." Inwardly she experienced a vast sense of relief. The biggest hurdle had been jumped.

Cole's gray gaze swept over her. "You'll be happy with that arrangement?"

"I think it will work." She pulled free of his assessing eyes and gazed down at the foaming wake several decks below. "Thank you, Cole."

"For what? Not forcing you to give up your work? I want you to be satisfied with the relationship, Kelsey. I realize you have a fear of giving up your job and your independence to come and live with me. I'm hoping that after a while you'll feel relaxed enough about the situation to risk it, but in the meantime I'm willing to make compromises."

Something in the way he said that caused her lips to lift in amusement. "You're being very generous," she assured him smoothly.

"I am," he agreed roughly. "And if you had any sense, witch, you wouldn't laugh at me because of it."

Suddenly contrite, she moved closer, reaching up to touch the side of his jaw. "I'm not laughing at you, Cole. I think I'm just greatly relieved that my job isn't going to be a problem." Her near-green eyes were wide with reassuring warmth.

Cole caught her fingers and kissed the tender heart of her palm. His eyes burned into hers. "I told you once I'd give you anything I could."

"I think you mean you'll give me anything you feel is good for me. There's a slight difference," she teased.

He let that pass, his intensity still engraved on his hard features. "There are other things that need to be considered, Kelsey."

"What things?" She was feeling too thankful for the unexpected concession to worry about what might be coming next.

"There's the possibility you could be pregnant."

The warmth in Kelsey's eyes turned to shock, and she dropped her fingers from the side of his face while she absorbed the implications of his statement.

Cole gave her a moment to respond, and when she didn't and merely continued to stand very still by the side of the rail staring out to sea, he went on determinedly.

"It's something we have to think about, Kelsey. On the two occasions I've made love to you I haven't taken any precautions. Unless you're on the pill...?" He left the question hanging.

Before stopping to think that it might be better to lie,

Kelsey found herself shaking her head. "No. No, I'm not using anything. There hasn't been any need, I mean there hasn't been anyone—" She broke off, angry at the way she was beginning to flounder.

Cole's hands closed over her shoulders and he pulled her back against the hard planes of his body. "I'm not complaining, honey," he murmured into her hair. "I like the fact that when you're in my arms you forget everything else. But it's something we should think about."

"I agree," she said fervently. "From now on we must be careful. Until we get back to the States there isn't much I can do, so I'll have to rely on your handling the details, won't I?" The tension in her must have communicated itself to Cole, because he began to knead her upper arms soothingly.

"I'll take care of everything," he said quietly. "But that's not the main problem. What we have to think about is the possibility that you already are pregnant."

"No."

"No, you're not?" he queried politely.

She shook her head quickly. "No, we won't think about the possibility that I'm pregnant. You have a policy of not concerning yourself with the future, remember? If there's anything on this earth that has 'future' written all over it, it's a baby. Therefore we will not deal in such iffy matters. Stockton's Second Law of Survival. The first, of course, being that we don't talk about the past. However, since I shall be left to deal with the future on my own, I expect you to take those precautions you spoke of a moment ago."

"Kelsey," he began huskily.

She straightened away from his hold and spun lightly around to confront him. Deliberately she summoned a brilliant smile. Knowing her eyes were probably not reflecting that brilliance, Kelsey tried to compensate with a tauntingly light tone of voice.

"Only the present, Cole. Remember? And right now I think I would like to dance."

She felt the hesitation in him, and he failed to respond to her beckoning smile.

"Kelsey, you can't just ignore this."

"Of course I can. You've taught me how to ignore a great deal. Come and dance with me, Cole.

"But, Kelsey..."

"This is our imitation honeymoon. Are you going to ruin it by being so deadly serious the whole time?"

"Damn it, woman, I want to talk about this!" he exploded tightly, refusing to budge as she tugged lightly on his wrist.

"But I don't want to talk about the future, Cole. It's all so uncertain, isn't it? Are you going to stand out here all night?"

"No," he gritted. "As a matter of fact, I think I'd like to go inside and have a stiff drink."

Kelsey wasn't quite certain how to take that, but she relaxed when he allowed her to lead him inside to one of the crowded lounges. And when she slipped into his arms on the dance floor, she told herself she could do what she had promised herself she would do. She would live life with Cole the way he chose to live it. She'd live by his rules.

Hours later, when he crushed her heavily down into the crisp sheets of his stateroom bunk, Cole told himself that he had got everything he wanted. Why the damned feelings of uncertainty wouldn't leave him alone, he couldn't understand. And, as always, just under the uncertainty lay the threat of panic.

Perhaps it was that buried threat that compelled him to wring the shuddering cries of satisfaction from Kelsey's lips over and over again that night. She gave herself without reservation, eagerly and with a delicious abandon that made him glory in his manhood. He derived an incredibly intense pleasure from the feel of her silky legs wrapped around his thighs. The peaks of her breasts were hard little berries that he nibbled with exquisite gentleness. And the warm moistness that flowed from the center of her desire welcomed his thrusting passion in a way that made him throb with an excitement that was more satisfying than anything he had ever known.

But when he awoke at dawn the next morning, Cole knew he hadn't managed to throttle that strange sense of unsureness.

It continued to needle him at odd moments throughout the day. After lunch he threw himself down on a lounger to watch Kelsey swim, and he found himself staring at her slender waist.

What if she was pregnant? He had begun taking precautions last night and he would honor his commitment to take care of her in that way. But that didn't answer the question of what was to be done if she already had conceived.

And she simply wouldn't discuss the issue.

Irritably Cole studied the sleek lines of the tangerine swimsuit Kelsey was wearing. He would feel very uncomfortable, far too visible and exposed, in anything that bright, but he liked the brilliant plumage on Kelsey. Of course, the suit was cut too low in the back and it didn't seem to have a built-in bra, but it was exciting to watch her in it.

Everything about Kelsey was satisfying and exciting, he was thinking when a white-jacketed steward walked through the crowd calling Kelsey's name.

"Miss Kelsey Murdock. Message for Kelsey Murdock."

Cole snapped his head around and frowned. Kelsey had just gone underwater. She wouldn't hear her name being called.

"I'll take it for her," Cole said calmly, extending his hand with a commanding air, which hopefully would cause the messenger to respond without thinking. "She's in the pool. It's all right. I'll give it to her."

"Okay," the steward said agreeably. "I was going to leave it under her door, but the guy who left the message said he'd already been unable to reach her on the phone. And he said it was urgent."

"Miss Murdock is spending the remainder of the cruise in my room," Cole informed him coolly. "Have any further messages transferred there."

The attitude of command worked, as it usually did, and the steward cheerfully pocketed the tip Cole gave him. Glancing toward the turquoise water to assure himself that Kelsey was still doing laps under the surface, he quickly ripped open the white envelope. The message inside had been taken by the ship's communications officer. It was from Walt Gladwin.

Kelsey, call ASAP. What's going on? Had message from Valentine. Request more details at once.

Gladwin

Cole reread the short message and then calmly shredded the piece of paper in his hands. Gladwin wasn't going to be allowed to interfere with this crucial week. Besides, the man deserved to stew in his office in San Jose. Cole was never going to absolve the other man of blame for having been the one to blithely send Kelsey into the dangerous situation on Cibola.

Getting to his feet, Cole deposited the shredded message in a nearby trash bin and then turned to glance back at the pool. Kelsey was just climbing up the ladder, her wet hair streaming behind her.

As he watched, Cole could see the outline of her sexy nipples as they pushed against the fabric of the tangerine suit. He wasn't the only male near the pool who noticed the enticing shape of her breasts, he realized at once.

Seizing an oversized towel from her lounger, he stalked forward to meet her at the edge of the pool. She blinked the water out of her eyes and smiled up at him as he approached.

"Something wrong, Cole?" she asked politely.

He knew he was glowering at her. "Cover yourself, woman. That suit is attracting too much attention."

She grinned recklessly, her eyes alight with mischief. "And you think yours isn't? I'll admit you look good in basic black," she told him, glancing down at the sleek black trunks he was wearing, "but I don't think it's the color that's attracting that redhead's eye."

Cole was astounded at the warmth he knew must be staining his cheekbones. He swore softly at the very idea that his body was capable of embarrassing him at his age. But he could feel the tightness in his loins and the pressure of the black swim trunks against his manhood.

"This," he informed Kelsey, "is all your fault." He grabbed the towel back from her and wrapped it around his lean hips, trying his best to look nonchalant. "If you hadn't come out of that pool wearing little more than a wet handkerchief this wouldn't have happened. You can damn well come on down to my stateroom and take care of the problem."

Kelsey giggled. "I can handle it right here."

Before he realized her intention, Cole felt her flatten her hands against his naked chest and push. An instant later he was sinking with a splash into the turquoise pool.

The thing about Kelsey, Cole told himself grimly as he resurfaced, was that even if he were able to overcome the odd feeling of uncertainty he experienced around her, he would never find her totally predictable. He saw her watching him from the edge of the pool and knew from the look in her eyes that she wasn't quite sure how he was going to take the playfulness."

"Nervous?" he drawled meaningfully. "Don't be. You solved the problem."

She relaxed back into teasing laughter. And quite suddenly Cole was vastly pleased with himself for being able to make her laugh.

The scene at the pool set the tone of their remaining time on board the ship. There was laughter during the days as they explored the ports of call and passion each night in Cole's stateroom.

There were also two more messages from Gladwin, both of which Cole managed to intercept before they reached Kelsey. He would probably have some explaining to do when they returned to California, Cole reminded himself occasionally, but that was in the future. No sense letting it spoil the present.

For the present was very good, indeed, and if he couldn't succeed in completely banishing the flickering moments of unease he had whenever Kelsey refused to discuss anything other than the present, Cole at least managed to keep the underlying panic at bay.

TEN

The idyllic week came to an end the moment Kelsey turned the key in the lock of her San Jose apartment. The phone was ringing violently.

"Oh, for heaven's sake!" she grumbled, tossing down her lightweight carryall and hurrying forward to pick up the receiver. Cole appeared in the doorway behind her, loaded down with his suitcase and her own. He stood for a few seconds curiously absorbing the interior as Kelsey answered the ringing summons.

"Walt!" she exclaimed after the initial hello. "Hey, wait a minute before you begin shouting at me. I just walked in the door. What? Yes, it was very exciting. Did Valentine tell you everything? He's absolutely charming, Walt. I liked him enormously." She paused as her boss fairly exploded in her ear. At last it began to dawn on Kelsey that this was not just a welcome-home call.

"I have one hell of a lot of questions for you, Kelsey Murdock. Stay right where you are. I'm coming over."

Walt slammed down the phone on his end, leaving Kelsey staring at her own instrument.

"He's very worked up over that business on Cibola," she explained slowly to Cole as he prowled her apartment. "He's on his way over here. He sounds furious and I can't figure out why." She chewed her lower lip. "I knew I should have done something more official about that whole mess. After all, I was representing Flex-Glad's interests."

"So was Valentine," Cole replied, shrugging. "And he knew a lot more about the local government than you did. As an off-islander you wouldn't have been able to accomplish much. I like your apartment, Kelsey."

She blinked at the abrupt change of topic. "Oh? Well, thanks. Maybe Valentine ran into some trouble trying to handle things on Cibola."

"Valentine can handle trouble. The only problem with this apartment is that it's wide open." Cole examined the window-locking mechanism. "You need better locks on everything. The ones you have are almost worthless. I suppose the first thing I'd better do is upgrade the security system. I should have done it a month ago."

"You've never seen my apartment before," Kelsey reminded him irritably. "How could you have known a month ago that my locks weren't the best?"

"Knowing you, it was a safe bet. You're not really much into security measures." Cole absently fingered the inexpensive lock on her front door.

"Well, I'll admit I wouldn't want to put up ten-foot-high walls around the place," Kelsey murmured, watching him curiously.

"You mean like the ones I have in Carmel. You've never liked my home, have you, Kelsey?" He glanced back at her over his shoulder. "You always made excuses not to have dinner with me there. The only time you came inside was that morning you discovered my name in your stepfather's computer."

Kelsey's expression softened as it occurred to her for the first time that her wariness of his home might have hurt him on some level. She got to her feet and walked across the room to put her arms around his neck. "I think I was afraid of getting trapped inside and never being allowed to leave," she confessed lightly.

Cole didn't respond to the lightness. His palms slid down the sides of her oversized white shirt and came to rest possessively on the snug-fitting denim that encased her hips. "That may have been a legitimate fear," he remarked wryly, bringing his mouth down on hers.

He had barely begun the kiss, when the angry roar of an expensive automobile engine filled the air. Kelsey pulled away reluctantly. "That will be Walt. With the Ferrari, it sounds like."

"Oh, by the way, Kelsey. About the story we give Gladwin..." Cole tossed out almost negligently.

"What do you mean, 'story'?" she demanded, startled.

"I just wanted to mention that Valentine intended to keep us out of his report as far as possible. The official line from him is that he caught some armed men going through his possessions on Cibola. Upon questioning them, he decided they were after the attaché case. He was going to let Gladwin take it from there. According to Valentine, you arrived on the island after the fracas was all over. And you came alone. I wasn't with you."

"But why?" Kelsey was dumbfounded.

"I'll explain it all later, okay? Trust me."

Kelsey clenched her teeth, telling herself that if she heard that request one more time she would probably come apart at the seams.

Her brow furrowed in angry tension, she went to open the door and found an irate Walt Gladwin on her doorstep.

"It's about time you got home. I've been trying to get in touch with you for days. Why didn't you respond to any of my messages, Kelsey? Did you think that when you're on vacation you aren't working for me, or something? For Pete's sake, I've been going nuts here trying to figure out what was going on."

"Come on in, Walt." Kelsey stepped back to allow the annoyed man inside. "And tell me what messages you're talking about. I never had any messages from you. Oh, and this is Cole Stockton," she added quickly as the two men surveyed each other with critical eyes.

"Stockton." Walt nodded curtly at the taller man and then turned back to Kelsey. "I sent three messages to the ship, not to mention trying to call you twice. It was obvious right away that I was never going to get you on the phone. Apparently you didn't spend much time in your own room," he added, sliding an annoyed glance at Cole.

"No, she didn't spend much time in her room. She spent most of her nights in mine," Cole said blandly.

"Cole, please," Kelsey gritted. "I'll handle this." Cole's possessiveness was going to be a problem on occasion, she knew, if not an actual source of embarrassment.

Cole ignored her with monumental indifference. He stood easily, watching Gladwin with chilled eyes. "I decided it was safer for her in my room. After all, working for a boss who sends her off into messy situations such as she apparently encountered on Cibola isn't good for a woman's health."

"What the devil is that supposed to mean?" Gladwin demanded furiously. "And just how much do you know about all this?"

"Cole, will you please stay out of this?" Kelsey begged, horrified at the way matters were rapidly escalating beyond her control. "Why don't you go fix us some coffee, or something?"

"She keeps the coffee next to the brandy," Gladwin tossed out with the air of a man who obviously knew his way around a woman's home. "You can't miss it."

"Both of you, stop it this minute!" Kelsey yelped, genuinely frightened now by the glacier cold in Cole's gray eyes.

"She told me that the man called 'Valentine' had his house searched by some armed thugs before she arrived. If she'd got to Cibola a little earlier, she might have been in the middle of things. I don't take kindly to a man who casually sends a woman off on little ventures like that," Cole went on conversationally.

"I don't particularly care how you take to me, Stockton. Kelsey works for me. I can send her where I want, when I want. Just who do you think you are, anyway?"

"The man who intercepted all your messages on board ship," Cole said politely.

"What messages?" Kelsey pleaded frantically. "Will someone please tell me what's going on? I didn't get any messages, Walt."

"That's because loverboy here apparently saw to it that you didn't," Walt shot back seethingly. He jammed his hands into his jacket pocket and glared at her. "I tried to reach you because, believe it or not, I would have liked to have had a report on exactly what happened. Do you realize I've had to call in the FBI? Ever since Valentine phoned and explained that things had got 'adventurous'—I believe that was the word he used—I've been running around like crazy."

"What's happened here, Walt?" Kelsey asked hurriedly. She'd get back to the matter of the intercepted messages later, she told herself. Right now a distraction was definitely called for, or she might find herself witness to more violence. There wasn't much doubt about which of the two men she'd be nursing afterward, either. Kelsey had seen enough of Cole's dangerous abilities to know Walt would be lucky to be able to crawl away from any battle between the two of them.

"I'll tell you what's going on here," Walt rasped, switching his glare back to her. "After Valentine gave me some names and information he said should be turned over to the FBI, I took his advice and called them in. They came down on Flex-Glad like a ton of bricks. Then two days ago Tom Bailey disappeared."

"Bailey? From the software planning department? Where did he go? Does the FBI suspect he might be the leak?"

"That's the current guess. From what we can piece together so far with Valentine's information it looks like Bailey was trying to sell those printouts to a representative of a not-so-friendly foreign power. He'd promised delivery several weeks ago, but he hadn't counted on the tight security Flex-Glad imposed here in corporate headquarters. But he did find out approximately when the printouts were due to arrive on Cibola."

"So he arranged to have the attaché case snatched on Cibola?" Kelsey asked uncertainly.

"The Bureau thinks he probably didn't know how to go about arranging that kind of thing himself. They suspect he simply told that representative of another country when the printouts were going to be delivered. The professionals took over from there." Gladwin ran a hand through his light-colored hair. "Valentine told me most of what went on, but he's a little hard to talk to at times. I was trying to get in touch with you in order to get the full story."

Cole interrupted coolly, "Just what did Valentine tell you?"

Gladwin shot him a fulminating glance. "Only that some armed thugs had come ashore and torn his place apart. He seemed more upset about that aspect of the situation than anything else."

"It was his home," Cole pointed out dryly.

"Yes, well, those printouts were worth a great deal more than his island home!"

"Maybe not to Valentine."

"Look, Stockton, will you just stay out of this? You're not involved as anything other than a nuisance, so I would appreciate it if you'd butt out."

"'Nuisance'?" Cole flicked an amused glance at Kelsey's tense face. "Just what did Valentine tell you?"

"Well, after he explained that his place had been searched but that the timing had been wrong—"

"'Wrong'?" Kelsey inserted curiously.

Gladwin nodded brusquely. "He explained that you hadn't yet delivered the attaché case. He caught the men responsible with the help of a friend and turned them over to the local authorities. I realize that by the time you arrived on Cibola everything was under control and we can't get our hands on those men who came looking for the printouts, much less prove that's what they were after, but that doesn't mean I didn't expect a full report from you. Kelsey, you were the only Flex-Glad employee on the scene. Valentine is hardly an employee, you know. You should have got back to me immediately."

Kelsey sent a questioning frown at Cole, who shrugged. He gave her a hard glance warning her that this was no time to dispute Valentine's story. She turned back to Walt.

"I'm sorry I didn't get in touch with you, Walt. Valentine told me he'd handle everything."

"Well, he did, I guess," Walt admitted peevishly. "But I still wanted to speak to you."

"I gather the FBI didn't feel compelled to talk to me, or did I miss some messages from them, too?" Kelsey narrowed her eyes as she looked over at Cole.

It was Walt who answered. "Valentine talked to them. Told them you couldn't add any further information, since the whole thing was over by the time you hit the island. The local agent said they'd get a statement from you when you returned to San Jose."

"I see." Kelsey wasn't sure what to say next.

Cole was not nearly so reticent. "If you've finished chewing her out for what wasn't her fault, why don't you run along. Kelsey and I would like to unpack and get settled. There's really not much else Kelsey can tell you, anyway."

Gladwin looked disconcerted. "But I haven't even talked to her yet!"

"It's true you've been monopolizing the conversation," Cole agreed.

"Look, Kelsey, we have a lot to discuss. Get rid of this guy, and then we can sit down and go over your report."

"Kelsey's still on vacation, in case you haven't noticed. If she sits down anywhere, you can bet I'll be right beside her."

Kelsey decided to act. The entire scene had gone far enough. "Walt, I feel a little disoriented. Give me a few hours to readjust to real life, okay? How about overnight? I'll be in your office first thing in the morning."

Gladwin sent one more infuriated glance at Cole and

then apparently decided discretion was more comfortable than insisting on his rights. It was becoming clear that Cole would be equally insistent and that he might be able to defend his rights as a lover more ruthlessly than Gladwin could defend his as Kelsey's employer.

"Eight o'clock tomorrow morning, Kelsey."

"I'll be there, Walt," she assured him quickly. She held the door for him as he stalked out. Shutting it with a groan of relief, she leaned back against it to confront Cole. The flicker of relief changed to simmering anger as she faced his implacable expression. "So you took it upon yourself to intercept messages meant for me?"

Cole didn't answer her immediately. He assessed her flashing eyes and then walked over to stare out the window. "I had to, Kelsey."

"Why?" The single word was clipped and loaded.

"I needed that time on board ship with you," he finally said simply. "I was afraid that if Gladwin got in touch, he'd insist you fly home at once. Even if I could convince you not to obey his summons, it was bound to distract you. I didn't want any distractions. That time was for us."

"But Cole, he's my employer!"

He spun around with the smoothness of a coiling snake. "And I'm your lover."

She ought to be protesting his arrogance, telling him exactly where his rights and privileges as a lover ended, letting him know she would not tolerate his interference in her life.

But as Kelsey stood staring at his hard, set face, she

read something more than arrogance in those usually unreadable eyes. Something close to desperation.

She was imagining things, she told herself. Cole had all the self-confidence in the world. He knew exactly what he wanted and he'd do whatever he had to in order to get it. Arrogance. Domineering, heavy-handed arrogance. That's all she could possibly see in those icy eyes.

But she had spent a very intimate week with him. They had been through a great deal of danger and passion together. Perhaps she really was getting to the point where she understood him on some levels. Maybe she shouldn't discount what her intuition was telling her.

"And as my lover you felt you had the right to keep Walt's messages from me?"

"We needed that time alone together, Kelsey," he insisted stubbornly.

"Why?"

"To establish the basis of our relationship!" he threw back roughly. "I wanted us to have time to get to know each other. Time apart from the world. You said yourself that being on board ship was like being in another world. I knew we'd have to come back and deal with real life soon enough. But I wanted us to come back united. Oh, hell, I'm not explaining this very well."

She thought about that. For the first time she wondered why a man who did not believe in the past or the future would make an effort to establish the groundwork for an affair. Affairs were, by definition, fleeting things, easily dissolved. Why wouldn't such a man simply take what she was obviously willing to give and be content. Her stomach knotted with a strange tension as she considered the ramifications of Cole's words. He was talking as though he were trying to build the basis for a real future. She wondered if he even realized what he was doing. Her poor stomach became even tenser as she allowed herself to wonder if Cole could eventually learn to believe not only in the future but in love.

"Cole Stockton, you can be absolutely infuriating. But the damage is done now. I'll be lucky to have a job tomorrow morning," she said with a sigh, sinking down onto the couch.

"Kelsey, I only did what I had to do."

"Uh, huh." Wisely she let that drop. Nothing she could say would convince him he shouldn't have kept those messages from her. "You never did like my job," she said wryly.

To her surprise he lifted his shoulder in an off-handed gesture of disinterest. "I think Gladwin's the kind of hustler who will take advantage of your loyalty to the firm, but I guess he's no worse than most other employers."

Kelsey's eyes opened wide in astonishment. "Well, that's a new line. Since when did you decide Gladwin's no worse than any other boss?"

Cole's mouth twisted ruefully. "Since I realized the two of you aren't particularly interested in each other on a nonbusiness level. Oh, Gladwin would probably take anything you offered, but you're not offering, and he's not going to make a grab for it. You're safe enough around him—at least when it comes to a physical relationship."

"Good grief! You determined all that just now?"

He came toward Kelsey, sitting down beside her. Cole's expression was very serious. "I still think you need someone to keep him from taking advantage of your willingness to work. But you'll have me around to do that now, won't you? I'll make certain he doesn't send you off on any idiotic delivery trips or require that you work weekends and nights. I think I can live with your job, Kelsey."

She bit off the sarcastic, "Gee, thanks," that sprang to her lips as she realized just how much that admission meant, coming from Cole Stockton. "I'm, uh, glad," she managed, not knowing quite what else to say. She seized on the other point that was plaguing her. "Tell me why Valentine kept us out of the story he gave Gladwin."

"That was mostly for my sake."

"Well?" she prompted when he didn't continue. "Why?"

"He was protecting my privacy," Cole explained simply.

"Why?" she pressed.

"Because the last thing I want to do is get mixed up with an investigation of any kind." He uncoiled from the couch and paced toward the kitchen.

Kelsey sprang up to follow him. "But, why, Cole?"

He was already running a glass of water for himself in the kitchen sink. He didn't look at her. "Because even the most casual investigations have a way of resurrecting things that are better off left buried. Take my word for it, Kelsey. It's easier this way."

Take my word for it. Trust me. Was she going to spend her whole life running up against this brick wall he'd built to guard his past, Kelsey wondered.

She answered her own question at once. No, she wouldn't be spending her life beating her head against his walls. She would only have to spend the short time he wanted her for an affair.

"All right, Cole," she agreed gently. "I'll take your word for it. I trust you."

He set the glass down on the counter with a snap and swooped across the kitchen, catching her up in his arms. His eyes were blazing with sudden desire.

"I was right about that time on the ship, wasn't I? It made a difference for us."

"Yes, Cole. It made a difference." Spearing her fingers through his hair, she lifted her face for his kiss. His mouth was fierce on hers. A week ago she would have read some of that near violence as an example of his determination to dominate her physically.

But for the second time that day she wondered if there wasn't something more beneath the surface of his actions. It seemed now as though he were somehow trying to reassure himself of her commitment.

Nonsense, Kelsey thought fleetingly. She had already given him everything he'd asked for. He could not possibly need any reassurance.

When he eventually lifted his mouth from hers, Cole did so reluctantly. "I'm going to have to go back to Carmel for the remainder of this week, honey. I have business to attend to, and I've got a lot of work to do, getting ready to shift files and records here to your apartment."

"I know, Cole." They had discussed this briefly on the return flight. Cole could not move in immediately. He had to arrange for the transfer of his business. "Mom and Roger are due home next Friday. I'll pick them up at the airport and drive them on down to Carmel."

"And on Sunday evening we'll come back to San Jose together," he concluded firmly.

"Yes."

He nibbled persuasively at the corner of her lips as he pulled her white shirt free of the jeans. "I'm going to miss having you in my bed this week." Cole stroked his palms up under the shirt until he found her breasts.

"Just think, no more having to squeeze the two of us into a narrow stateroom bunk," she teased lightly.

"I rather liked the squeezing."

"That's because you're bigger than I am. You always wound up with the lion's share of the bed."

"Size has it privileges. What sort of bed do you have here?" He tasted the curve of her throat with a questing tongue.

"That's a leading question if I ever heard one," she complained, nestling closer as his palms tantalized her nipples.

"So lead me on," he invited in a husky growl.

Friday afternoon Kelsey met her mother and stepfather at the airport as scheduled and spent the drive to

Carmel delicately trying to explain about her relationship with Cole.

"He'll be coming over for dinner tonight," Kelsey said at one point after going through a long explanation of how he had accompanied her on the cruise.

"And you'll be going back to his home afterward, is that what you're trying to tell us?" Amanda Evans asked cheerfully.

"I think you've got the picture, Mom."

"When's the wedding?" Roger demanded easily.

"It's a subject we don't discuss," Kelsey said calmly.

"Well," Roger mused, "even if Cole doesn't discuss such things, I don't think I'll have to get out the shotgun. Stockton's a man who will honor his obligations, one way or another."

Kelsey slanted a speculative glance at her charming gentleman of a stepfather and smiled, but she said nothing. Whatever that business was involving Cole and Roger, there didn't appear to be any anger or bitterness between the two men. Just secrets.

"The two of you look marvelous," she noted, opting to change the subject as she changed lanes on the freeway. The Friday traffic was worse than usual tonight. "I gather New Zealand agreed with you."

"Wonderful place," Amanda enthused excitedly. "Roger and I are thinking of going back next year, aren't we, dear?" She leaned forward over the front seat to smile at her husband. Her short, stylish gray hair emphasized the wide hazel-green eyes Kelsey had inherited. Amanda Evans was a trim, outgoing woman who was thoroughly enjoying the new lifestyle her money had bought her. It showed in the way she wore her expensive designer fashions with obvious delight and in the laughter in her smile.

"I'm holding out for that cruise to Tahiti we discussed," Roger said, giving his wife an affectionate grin. His patrician features relaxed easily when he smiled at Amanda. "Just look at what a cruise did for Kelsey. She looks terrific."

"I don't think the cruise is responsible for that," Amanda murmured. "I think that's love."

"Speaking of the cruise," Roger went on conversationally. "How did your little side trip to Cibola go? Did you find your eccentric genius?"

Kelsey drew a deep breath. "Thereby hangs a tale," she said. And then she told them exactly what had happened during the twenty-four hours on Cibola.

When Cole strolled through the front door of the Evans home that evening wearing the familiar black pullover and black slacks he'd worn the fateful night Kelsey had tried to end their relationship, Roger greeted him with a drink and a demand for details.

"I want to hear all about Cibola, too," Amanda had warned as she swept in from the kitchen carrying a tray of herbed caviar puffs. "Sit down, Cole, and tell us everything. We've already heard Kelsey's story."

Cole's eyes narrowed as he looked at Kelsey over the top of her mother's head. Having no difficulty at all in reading the disapproval of his gaze, Kelsey smiled brilliantly and came forward to brush his mouth in a light kiss of greeting. She moved away before he could pull her closer.

"I told them all about it, Cole. The real story. And I explained that Valentine has already given Gladwin a slightly different version." She picked up her glass of wine and sat down beside her mother on the cream-colored sofa. The slim lines of her narrowly cut turquoise dress made a bright splash of color against the light background. She lifted her chin with just the smallest hint of assertiveness as Cole continued to frown at her.

"It might have been better if we'd all stuck by Valentine's version. For the sake of consistency, if nothing else," Cole said pointedly.

"I can keep secrets from some people but not from the ones I love," Kelsey told him with a quiet calm she was far from feeling.

"Kelsey never could abide secrets," Amanda interjected nonchalantly. "She can keep them when she has to, but she hates having to do it any more than necessary. And her natural curiosity drives her crazy when she knows someone is keeping a secret from her."

"Not unlike her mother," Roger put in smoothly before Cole could respond. He turned back to the younger man. "So since we know all, Cole, you might as well fill us in on some of the gory details. I must say, I'm very glad Kelsey took you along on that little jaunt. Just how did you and Valentine smoke out the two thugs in his house? Kelsey was a bit vague on that point."

Cole surrendered to the inevitable, relaxing as he sipped the drink Roger had fixed for him. "Fortunately Valentine had a few tricks up his sleeve. The dicey part was the next morning when Kelsey decided to get involved. I'd given her strict instructions to wait in the cave."

"No, you didn't," Kelsey felt obliged to protest. "You were gone when I awoke. I merely went looking for you."

Cole gave her a wry glance. "You've already told the tale from your standpoint. How about letting me give it from my point of view?"

"Because I get the feeling it's going to be decidedly biased!"

"Listen to this, Amanda," Roger said, chuckling. "Their first argument and they're not even married yet."

Kelsey felt the warmth rush into her cheeks. To cover her sudden restlessness she got to her feet. "I've explained about marriage, or rather the lack thereof, Roger. Remember? Now if you'll excuse me, I'll let Cole give you his no-doubt-male-oriented view of the story while I go check on the lamb marinade." She paused a moment longer to throw Cole a cool look. "And for the record you can bet this isn't our first argument."

She swept out of the room with a flourish, and didn't realize her mother had followed until she came to a halt in the elegant white-and-chrome kitchen and found Amanda right behind her.

"I take it Cole would have preferred you not tell us the full story of what happened on Cibola, hmm?" Amanda poked at the apricot marinade on the lamb chops.

"Cole's big on keeping secrets," Kelsey said, opening the refrigerator door to pull out the salad.

"And you think that makes him unique?" Amanda asked, amused. "Roger's got a few of his own."

In spite of herself, Kelsey shot a quick, questioning glance at her mother. "Serious ones?"

"He thinks they are," Amanda said gently. "He's sharing a secret with Cole, but he'd be traumatized if he thought I knew about it."

Very slowly Kelsey set the crystal bowl full of salad greens down on the counter and turned to face her mother. "And you do know about it?"

Amanda cocked an eyebrow at her daughter's very sober expression. "I get the feeling you know about it, too. What happened? Did Roger put the little matter of his debt to Cole on the computer?"

"Mom, I didn't mean to pry," Kelsey explained hurriedly. "I was just browsing through the computer to see how Roger was doing, and I found the file. I...I was shocked. I couldn't imagine why Roger would be paying Cole a thousand dollars a month."

"I found the file when it was still being kept in Roger's accounting books, before he transferred it to the computer." Amanda took the salad bowl over to the other side of the counter and reached for the dressing she had prepared earlier.

"And you went through it?"

"Well, of course, darling. What wife wouldn't?"

Kelsey grimaced. "Maybe the men are right to keep secrets from us."

"Nonsense. They don't do it because we can't be

trusted. At least men like Roger and Cole don't keep secrets for that reason. Deep down they know we wouldn't betray them. We may be deeply curious about them, but we are also intensely loyal to them."

"Then why...?"

"Because they try to protect us, naturally." Amanda tossed the salad with a theatrical air.

"'Protect us'?"

"Certainly. Also themselves."

"Mom, I don't understand," Kelsey protested.

"Well, take Roger, for instance. He's hiding that debt to Cole because he couldn't bear to have me find out his financial status isn't as strong as he'd like it to be. He lost a great deal of money in the stock market last year and that loan was to cover his losses. It was either ask Cole for the loan or ask me. His handwritten notes were very explicit."

"He couldn't bring himself to ask you?"

"He's afraid I'll not only worry about the money but also think less of him for having taken the heavy losses."

"It's all wrapped up with his ego?"

"Kelsey, dear, almost everything a man does is somehow wrapped up with his ego. Male egos are very fragile things. But men seem to function to a large extent on them. Along with a few other basic instincts and drives such as possessiveness, protectiveness and pride."

"I'm learning," Kelsey sighed. "I know Cole can certainly be overly possessive, overly protective and overly arrogant. And he's always insisting that I trust him."

"Do you?"

Kelsey flung out her hand in a helpless gesture. "For some strange reason that utterly defeats me, I do."

"Well, in that case there's nothing to worry about, is there?" her mother said with a grin. "As long as you can trust a man the rest is merely a challenge."

Kelsey burst out laughing as she went across the tiled floor to hug her mother. "When did you pick up all this feminine wisdom, Mom?"

"Unfortunately it only comes with age. Believe me, I'd have given a great deal to have had it when I was younger. Now are those chops ready to go under the broiler?"

"They're ready."

The meal was a pleasant success, with the conversation moving on from the events on Cibola to Amanda's and Roger's experiences in New Zealand. Kelsey would have enjoyed the homecoming meal far more, however, if she hadn't been intensely aware of Cole's frequent, searching glances.

They came at odd moments during dinner. She'd pass the salad bowl to him and find him studying her. Or she'd ask for the butter dish and have it handed to her along with a speculative gleam in a pair of gray eyes. After dinner there were more such looks, and they made her uneasy. She began to lose some of her bright, charming mood.

Kelsey didn't think anyone noticed she was becoming increasingly quiet until her mother said sympathetically, "You look a little tired, dear. Hard week?"

"There was a lot to catch up on after that Caribbean cruise. I had to put in a lot of overtime." Kelsey heard herself use work as an excuse for her more silent mood and grew even more uneasy. That was the excuse she had used to explain her attitude that night she had decided to tell Cole goodbye. It was as phony then as it was tonight. In both cases it was Cole who was responsible for her tension.

"That probably explains why I wasn't able to reach you on the phone Thursday evening until after eight," Cole said deliberately.

Kelsey stirred with a tinge of restlessness. "Yes." He had called her at eight-thirty that evening, but he had never mentioned until now that he'd tried earlier. She found herself gnawing gently on her lower lip and stopped at once. She was not going to let him make her tense like this. It was ridiculous.

But the atmosphere between them continued to vibrate with an escalating sense of danger. By the time she kissed her mother good-night and allowed Cole to lead her outside into the chilly darkness, Kelsey was feeling very strained.

They walked in silence down the private road that led to Cole's walled fortress. At the heavy wrought-iron gate, Cole entered a code into the computerized lock and stood silently aside, waiting for her to step into the garden.

As she hesitated and then brushed past him, Kelsey felt the tightly balanced tension in his body and suddenly realized she was not the only one on edge tonight. Cole was as remote and wary as he had ever been around her.

The gate clanged shut with a solid sound behind her, and Kelsey turned to glance back at it. In the light of the well-lit garden she found Cole gazing down at her.

"You were right about one thing," he said coolly. "Once inside the walls, you can't get back out."

"Cole, please don't tease me."

"But it's true, Kelsey." He took her arm and led her toward the front door. "Oh, you'll be able to come and go in a physical sense. But in another sense I could never let you go free."

She tried a tremulous smile. "Your possessive instincts are showing."

"I never knew I had any before I met you," he countered with deadly seriousness. He unlocked the front door and guided her down the hall to the living room. Without a word he escorted her to one of a pair of rattan chairs that faced the ocean. Then he paced silently across the room to pour two glasses of cognac.

Kelsey accepted one of the snifters with an odd sense of déjà vu. This was the kind of glass from which she had been drinking brandy that crucial night in her mother's home. She sipped carefully, her gaze on the darkened ocean that surged beyond the wrought-iron fence.

"Kelsey?" Cole didn't sit down in the other chair. Instead he moved to stand near the window, his back to her.

"Yes, Cole?"

"I've been doing a lot of thinking this past week."

Kelsey felt the faint trembling of the glass in her hand and knew it was due to the distinct tremor in her fingers. Oh, God, she had been right to be aware of tension in the atmosphere. Something was badly wrong. What had happened to Cole during the past week, she wondered frantically. Fear for the fate of her newfound love coursed through her. With a fierce effort she kept her voice calm.

"Have you, Cole?"

"We need to think about the commitment we're making by deciding to live together."

Kelsey's stomach tightened, but from somewhere she found the courage to say very evenly, "There's no need to think of our relationship in terms of commitment, is there? We're only dealing with the present, after all. If you—" She broke off to moisten her lower lip. "If you change your mind about our arrangement...I mean, you're perfectly free, Cole."

She thought the controlled tension in him went up another notch.

"Am I perfectly free?"

"I doubt there's a person on the face of this earth who could make you do anything you don't wish to do, Cole."

"Not even you?"

"Least of all me," she tried to say lightly.

He braced one hand against the window frame and lifted his glass to his mouth with the other. He was still staring intently out into the night as if he could see something she could not. "That shows how little you understand our situation, Kelsey."

She swallowed the fear that was threatening to choke her and tried to replace it with anger. "I don't know why you're choosing to go melodramatic on me all of a sudden. I thought everything was very clear-cut between us. All the ground rules have been worked out, remember? We're doing this exactly the way you wanted it. No past and no future. We take things on a day-by-day basis."

"And if I decide I don't like that kind of arrangement?"

"Then you're free to leave, aren't you?" she tossed back. "This is the way you wanted it, Cole."

He took a long drag on the brandy. "For someone who was once very big on long-term commitment, you've certainly changed your tune."

"I suppose I've learned from you," she retorted with savage spirit.

"What would you say if I asked you to marry me, Kelsey?" The question was ground out in a stark, steel-edged tone.

She caught her breath, struggling for the answer. "I'd say no. I'd *have* to say no." *Because it wouldn't be what you wanted,* she added silently to herself.

"And if it turns out you're pregnant?" he demanded grittily.

"I'm not. I found out for certain this past week. It was sweet of you to be concerned, Cole, but you really don't have to worry about that aspect of the situation any longer."

For the second time since she had known Cole Stockton, Kelsey found herself totally unprepared for the sensation of controlled violence that ripped through the room. As if in a dream, she watched him twist around with feral grace and slam the glass he had been holding on an end table. It met the hard surface with such force that the delicate stem snapped. Fragrant brandy spilled out on the table. The crackle of broken glass stunned Kelsey, but Cole hardly seemed aware of it.

"'Sweet of me to be concerned.' *Sweet* of me! My God, woman, haven't you learned yet there is nothing remotely *sweet* about the way I feel toward you?"

Instinctively Kelsey got to her feet, poised to run, as he stalked toward her. "Cole, wait, you don't understand!"

"Don't give me that bit about not understanding. You're the one who's missed something along the way. I'm not going to let you treat our relationship as a short-term affair, Kelsey Murdock. You belong to me now, and you'll belong to me fifty years hence. You've made a commitment and you're going to honor it. We're talking long-range, lady. We're talking about the future. And I'm finished with listening to you try to avoid that particular topic. There's no way you can run from me, Kelsey. Or from our future. It exists. Tonight I'm going to make you admit it."

ELEVEN

She wasn't going to run this time. Cole realized that almost immediately. Kelsey was physically poised for flight, but he was hunter enough to know from the look in her eyes that she wasn't going to flee.

"It wouldn't do you any good, anyway," he rasped as he moved a few steps closer.

"I know," she affirmed gently.

His eyes slitted warningly. "If you did try to run I'd have you before you got to the door."

"You don't have to tell me that, Cole. I've seen you move. I could never outrun you."

"I'm going to take you into my bed and keep you there until you realize that you belong there tonight, tomorrow night and every other night."

She said nothing, but she didn't move. Cole deliberately stalked to a point only a hand's reach away and halted. Kelsey faced him with wariness but no real fear. He searched her expression. "You're not afraid of me, are you?"

"Should I be?"

"I'm going to revise this entire relationship," he declared vehemently. "Doesn't that make you nervous?"

"We've been doing everything your way from the beginning, haven't we?" she countered.

He shook his head at the ludicrousness of her response. "You've fought me every inch of the way."

"You've won every battle." It was a simple statement, not an accusation. "Got everything you wanted."

Anguish shot through him. "Kelsey, I never wanted it to be war between us!"

"Why not? War is an art you know well, isn't it?"

Panic flared deep inside. Cole felt as though it would strangle him. He'd never experienced anything like it. It seized him by the throat and wrenched at his guts. And it took every ounce of willpower he had ever possessed to control it just to the point where only his hands shook.

"What do you know of that?" he heard himself whisper fiercely.

"Very little," she admitted calmly. "But no one could watch you or Valentine for any length of time and not know that at some time in your past you were warriors."

She knew. Or she had guessed. She had seen the past in him.

"That's why you won't talk about the future, isn't it?" he charged roughly. "That's the reason you no longer care about a long-term commitment. The reason you won't marry me. You'll let yourself indulge in an affair with me, but you're no longer interested in any future with a man who might have blood on his hands."

"Cole, listen to me."

"It's too late, Kelsey," he gritted, closing the small distance between them. Deliberately he reached out to place his hands on her shoulders. "You're going to have to learn to live with these hands on you." He used his thumbs to force up her chin. It seemed to Cole that her eyes had never been closer to true green than they were in that moment. He could feel the shimmering tension in her and see the faint tremor of her soft mouth. "God, Kelsey, there's no way on earth I could keep my hands off you. I want everything. All of you. And that includes your future."

He was expecting anything but the tender smile that curved her lips. Kelsey lifted her hands, her cinnamon-tipped nails sliding around the collar of his khaki shirt. "You can only have that if you're willing to give it in return," she murmured.

He shuddered heavily and wrapped her against him, burying his face in the compelling scent of her hair. "I've told you over and over I'll give you everything I can."

"I wasn't sure you really knew what that meant," she admitted gently. "You always seemed to talk in terms of making me a well-kept mistress."

He closed his eyes. "I suppose I thought that was all I had to offer. I wanted you so badly and I didn't know how to hold you. Kelsey, please say you'll marry me."

"I'll marry you," she breathed against his shoulder.

His hands tightened on her. It wasn't enough, Cole

realized. He wanted something else. "Why?" he finally asked boldly.

"Because I love you, of course. What other reason could there possibly be?"

That, Cole realized, was what had been missing. "You love me?" he repeated uncertainly. Even though he had the words from her, he didn't quite dare to believe them. "You *love* me, Kelsey?" He raised his head to look down at her, needing confirmation of this more than he had needed anything else in his life.

"I love you, Cole."

"Just like that?" he asked dazedly, remembering vaguely that he had asked that question in almost the same way on Cibola when she had given herself to him after the battle at Valentine's house.

"Just like that." She smiled, clearly remembering the prior occasion. "Just like that."

"In spite of what I might have been in the past?" He had to know, Cole told himself. He had to be certain.

She brushed his lips with the tips of her fingers. "The past is no longer important, Cole. Whatever it was, you've closed the door on it. I trust you to keep it closed."

"Oh, Kelsey," he groaned. "I love you."

"I believe you," she whispered against his mouth. "You've never lied to me."

"Kelsey...." He couldn't say anything more. Anything coherent, that is. Cole swept her up into his arms, violently aware of the warmth of her thigh as it reached him through the turquoise silk.

She cradled her head against his shoulder as he carried her down the hall to his bedroom. The door of the darkened room stood open and he walked through it, leaving the lights off. Then he put Kelsey down in the middle of the wide bed and stood for a moment looking at her in the pale moonlight.

Beyond the wall of windows the surf crashed in counterpoint to the throb of his own pulse. Cole saw the smile of feminine warmth and welcome on Kelsey's lips and realized he was shivering from a combination of physical desire and emotional need.

"You are the only one, Kelsey," he tried to explain as he shrugged out of his clothing. "The only one who can give me what I've been needing for so long." Naked at last, he came down beside her in a heated rush, gathering her close. "I didn't even know I needed love before you came into my life. I thought I had provided myself with everything a man like me could want."

Kelsey felt the surge of hunger that went far deeper than physical desire in him, and she stroked the hard planes of his back. "I love you, Cole."

"Just keep saying it. I'll never be able to hear it enough. Oh, Kelsey, I love you so much. When I realized you weren't even willing to discuss a future between us I nearly panicked. Lord, woman, I'm not accustomed to panic. I'm not even used to this god-awful uncertainty that's been plaguing me since I met you."

He growled the last words into her throat, his hands on the fastenings of the thin silk dress. Kelsey moaned softly as he stripped it from her with a long, sensuous movement that left her completely nude.

"So soft and warm and inviting," he whispered. His

palms slid possessively along the curves of her body, finding all the secret places that responded so readily to his touch.

Kelsey arched against him, drawing a fierce groan from his lips. Enthralled with the response, she trailed her fingertips down his back, pausing to clench them urgently into the lean flesh of his buttocks before moving to cradle the throbbing evidence of his desire.

"I love the feel of you," he muttered thickly. "And the scent of you. I think I'm addicted." He tasted the skin of her breasts and then went on to sample the silk of her stomach. Lower he moved, nipping with exciting gentleness along the delicate inside of her thigh. His fingers stroked the flowering heart of her until she cried out for him.

"Cole!"

Kelsey clung to his shoulders, pulling him up along the length of her and imprisoning him within the circle of her legs.

He came to her swiftly, as though he, too, could wait no longer for the throbbing union of their bodies. Kelsey gasped as he surged into her, filling her completely. And then she once again surrendered willingly to the mind-spinning rhythm of the passion they generated together.

When the pulsing climax overtook them they called each other's names over and over again until they plummeted as one into the depths of the bedding. Damp and languorous and content with a heavy warmth flooding her, Kelsey lay curled against Cole, her palm resting lightly on his chest.

"Kelsey," he finally said quietly. "I want to tell you."

"No, Cole. There's no need." She knew at once what he was going to talk about.

"I think there is. I don't want any more secrets between us."

She raised her head and smiled down at him. "Keep your secrets, Cole. I don't need them."

"Are you still afraid of them?"

"No."

He nodded, his eyes holding hers. "Then I can tell you."

She realized he had to talk now. Gently she touched the side of his face. "And then we'll close the door again and leave it closed."

Cole took a deep breath and began to talk. There in the darkness he told her what it had been like in that special unit of the military in Southeast Asia. He explained the remote, controlled facade he had developed to keep himself together emotionally when he was sent out on the top-secret missions that so often culminated in violence. He explained succinctly how that remote, carefully controlled wall had become more than a facade. It had become a part of him. And when he left the military, he continued to take the dangerous jobs that now paid so very well. The inner walls protected him.

"And then one day they weren't enough," Cole said evenly. "I wanted out. I wanted to start over. So I just disappeared. As far as the people I worked for are concerned, I never came back from my last mission. It seemed simpler that way." He stirred a little, folding

Kelsey closer. "No one seems to have cared. As far as I can tell no one bothered to go looking for me. They just wrote me off as a disposable commodity that had been all used up."

"So you came to Carmel and started over," Kelsey concluded, soothing him with her hands.

"And built a few more walls," he said, grimacing. "Walls that made you wary of me and of my home."

"I understand them now."

"Kelsey, there aren't any more barriers between us, are there? I love you."

She heard the raw truth in the husky words and smiled up at him as he leaned over her.

"No more barriers, Cole. And we don't need to concern ourselves with the past. We have a future now."

"Speaking of which, we must remember to invite Valentine to the wedding."

"Absolutely. Something tells me he'll be here with bells on."

"Valentine with bells on may be more than Gladwin can handle," Cole mused. Then his brief amusement faded. "Everything's really okay, sweetheart?"

"Everything's perfect," she said, gently laying the remnants of his uncertainty to rest. "And now that we've discussed the past and the future, I think it's time to consider the present."

"My pleasure," he growled. "Right now I'm very interested in the present." His mouth closed over hers in a kiss that sealed their love for all time.

ONE NIGHT
WILLA LONGWORTH
FOUND A FORTUNE...
AND A MAN

ANN MAJOR

Wild Enough For Willa

What does a woman do when she finds cold hard
cash at her feet? With a family against her, a son to
nourish and a passion to extinguish, Willa did what
any woman would do—she took the money and ran.

But the past was at her heels in the form of
dangerously handsome Luke McKade—a man who
would follow her to the ends of the earth and make
her pay for her sins. A man who had demons…and
a fierce need for Willa's heart and soul.

"Want it all? Read Ann Major." —Nora Roberts

On sale December 2000
wherever paperbacks are sold!

MIRA®

Visit us at www.mirabooks.com

MAM623

In a game of murder and deception,
is blind faith enough?

CHRISTIANE HEGGAN

BLIND FAITH

When Jonathan Bowman, a loving husband and father, disappears,
his wife instinctively turns to her best friend for help. Kelly Robolo
has seen everything in her years as an investigative reporter.
Now she must use all of that experience to help her friend.
When a charred body is identified as Jonathan's, Kelly suspects
it's a setup. Philadelphia cop Nick McBride suspects that same
thing. But the question is why? Soon, Nick and Kelly's suspicions
are luring them into a desperate and dangerous game where
blind faith leads straight into terror....

"A master at creating taut, romantic suspense."
—*Literary Times*

Available January 2001 wherever paperbacks are sold!

If you enjoyed what you just read,
then we've got an offer you can't resist!

Take 2
bestselling novels FREE!
Plus get a FREE surprise gift!

A glorious tapestry of love and war,
where the fiercest battleground lies within the heart...

GOLDEN PARADISE

A brilliant scholar, Lisaveta Lazaroff is both beautiful and
outspoken, an independent woman who refuses to play by
the rules that govern men and society. A bold attempt to ride
through the Turkish desert alone nearly ends her life, until she
is rescued by Prince Stefan Bariatinsky, a man whose passions
are as intense as the battles he wages. His only weakness lies
in a woman who challenges him for the one thing
he has never lost—his proud heart.

SUSAN JOHNSON

Available January 2001 wherever paperbacks are sold!

Visit us at www.mirabooks.com

MSJ854

Merline Lovelace

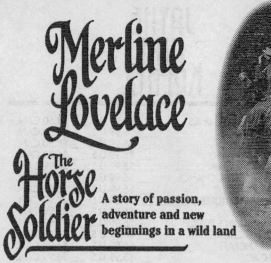

The Horse Soldier

A story of passion, adventure and new beginnings in a wild land

She came looking for her husband...

Determined to locate her missing husband, Julia Bonneaux makes a dangerous journey to the Wyoming Territory. But at Fort Laramie she comes face-to-face with Major Andrew Garrett: the dashing rogue she had secretly married seven years before...and the man she thought was dead all these years.

And found the man she loved.

Time has eased the pain of Andrew's months in a Confederate prison—but not the memory of Julia. When she asks for his help, Andrew is torn between duty and desire. With his career—and his heart—in jeopardy, he must choose between the misunderstandings of the past and the promise of a new beginning.

Merline Lovelace "writes with humor and passion..."
—*Publishers Weekly*

On sale January 2001 wherever paperbacks are sold!

JAYNE ANN KRENTZ

66595	BETWEEN THE LINES	___ $6.99 U.S.	___ $8.50 CAN.
66640	TEST OF TIME	___ $6.99 U.S.	___ $8.50 CAN.
66639	JOY	___ $6.99 U.S.	___ $8.50 CAN.
66563	CALL IT DESTINY	___ $5.99 U.S.	___ $6.99 CAN.
66555	THE FAMILY WAY	___ $5.99 U.S.	___ $6.99 CAN.
66524	GHOST OF A CHANCE	___ $5.99 U.S.	___ $6.99 CAN.
66494	THE COWBOY	___ $5.99 U.S.	___ $6.99 CAN.
66462	THE ADVENTURER	___ $6.99 U.S.	___ $7.99 CAN.
66437	THE PIRATE	___ $6.99 U.S.	___ $7.99 CAN.
66315	A WOMAN'S TOUCH	___ $6.99 U.S.	___ $7.99 CAN.
66270	LADY'S CHOICE	___ $6.99 U.S.	___ $7.99 CAN.
66158	WITCHCRAFT	___ $5.99 U.S.	___ $6.99 CAN.
66148	LEGACY	___ $5.99 U.S.	___ $6.99 CAN.

(limited quantities available)

TOTAL AMOUNT	$_____
POSTAGE & HANDLING	$_____
($1.00 for one book; 50¢ for each additional)	
APPLICABLE TAXES*	$_____
TOTAL PAYABLE	$_____

(check or money order—please do not send cash)

To order, complete this form and send it, along with a check or money order for the total above, payable to MIRA Books®, to: **In the U.S.:** 3010 Walden Avenue, P.O. Box 9077, Buffalo, NY 14269-9077; **In Canada:** P.O. Box 636, Fort Erie, Ontario L2A 5X3.

Name:_____
Address:_____ City:_____
State/Prov.:_____ Zip/Postal Code:_____
Account Number (if applicable):_____
075 CSAS

*New York residents remit applicable sales taxes.
Canadian residents remit applicable
GST and provincial taxes.